COSMIC RIDDLE

Dr. Lem wiped his face; it was glistening with sweat. "It's not bravery which kept me here, but obstinacy. Once upon a time I had this ambition, to unravel the mystery of Yan. And now it's turned out that the mystery hasn't been a mystery for years, and the solution's only been kept from me by an ingenious trick played on this informant. I feel cheated! I want to do something to compensate."

He hesitated. "And I have learned to love this planet."

"A field has been detected," said the informant. "The rain of meteorites on Kralgak has reduced by forty per cent—by forty-four per cent—by forty-nine per cent—it is extrapolated that the meteorites will cease completely in one minute twenty-two seconds from the mark. Mark."

"After all your work with the Mutine Epics," Dr. Lem said, "have you any clear idea what the dramaturge was trying to do?"

"Yes," Marc said. "Control the universe."

Also by John Brunner
Published by Ballantine Books:

DOUBLE, DOUBLE

THE INFINITIVE OF GO

THE LONG RESULT

PLAYERS AT THE GAME OF PEOPLE

THE SHEEP LOOK UP

SHOCKWAVE RIDER

STAND ON ZANZIBAR

THE WHOLE MAN

CATCH A FALLING STAR

BEDLAM PLANET

THE DRAMATURGES OF YAN

JOHN BRUNNER

A Del Rey Book

BALLANTINE BOOKS • NEW YORK

A Del Rev Book
Published by Ballantine Books

ISBN 0-345-30677-5

Manufactured in the United States of America

First Ballantine Books Edition: December 1982

Cover art by Darrell K. Sweet

I

ACROSS THE NIGHT the Ring of Yan arched like a silver bow, shedding the small bright fire-arrows of meteors into the upper air. Tired, but with so much tension in his brain he knew he would not yet be able to sleep— and unwilling, unless he was driven to it, to resort to his repose-inducer—Dr Yigael Lem discarded his formal Earthsider clothes in favour of a Yannish webweave gown and reed sandals, and walked out on his verandah to contemplate the sight he customarily relied on to pacify his thoughts. Madame de Pompadour, the pet chubble who had accompanied him to seven systems, had expected him to retire and accordingly had settled down in the dormicle to await his arrival. On realising he had gone elsewhere she gave a brief squawk of complaint, but ultimately gathered the energy to come and join him. She moved stiffly. She, like her owner, was getting old.

The air was mild with the promise of spring, and the earliest of his famous i blossoms were starting to show. A few years ago he had decided to tinker with the faulty gene in the original species which sometimes caused it to revert to the wild state, its flowers mere

1

balls of characterless green fluff, and achieved spectacular success—more by luck than skill, he always insisted when someone tried to compliment him on what he'd done, because although he had had to study physical medicine as a young man and graduated with distinction in gene-repair, he had not practised the technique for decades.

Now his garden was bordered by a hedge of unparalleled magnificence, from which even Speaker Kaydad had condescended to accept a cutting. Under the pale radiance of the Ring the buds on their tall segmented stalks looked like polished skulls, ready to open their jaws and utter indescribable statements of fragrance.

Convinced he wasn't going anywhere else for the moment, Pompy lay down and began to croon contentedly to herself, a curling question-mark of fur on the smooth tiles of the verandah. Occasional sounds drifted from nearby houses: a child's half-hearted cry for attention, laughter, the plaintive whistle of someone experimenting with a Yannish flute. But it was late now, and under these few surviving indices of wakefulness he could hear, quite plainly, the rushing of the great river Smor.

His home was on the crest of the highest rise in the neighbourhood. From opposite ends of this curved verandah he could look out over both the enclave of the Earthsiders—dominated by the go-board and by the dome of the informat—and also the native city Prell, spined by the black river running between the stone-paved ribs of its streets. Gloglobes bobbed on the bows of barges moored at the Isum Quay, like luminous fruit on branches stirred by the wind. One revealed to him the unmistakable outline of a *kortch,* the coffin-like case in which a Yannish baby born today or yesterday was to be transported away from its mother: upstream to Liganig, or along the coast to Frinth. There were good reasons why the Yanfolk were not deep-water sailors . . . or at least not nowadays. But they relied a great deal on river and coastal trade.

I ought to know whose child that is. A birth is an event among the Yanfolk.

But even as the words formed inside his head, they were driven aside by others, peculiarly sinister.

I wonder whose place it's due to take.

Instantly he was angry with himself. That wasn't a fair way to think of *shrimashey.* Surely he, as a psychologist, should be detached, should refrain from making human value-judgments about alien customs. In any case, it wouldn't be anybody he knew whose place was taken; the equation would be balanced elsewhere, at Liganig or Frinth or still further distant from Prell.

When they celebrate a birth, though, it's so ironical to realise they're also holding a wake, displaced in time—a wake for someone not yet dead, whom they haven't met!

Determinedly, he sought to thrust notions of that sort to the back of his mind. It was in vain. They kept recurring, like a shadow cast over his thoughts. Indeed the impression of being overshadowed was so strong, he jerked around without intending to, as though there might actually be a silent menace trying to catch him unawares from behind, and his eyes were seized and held by the tall crystal pillars silhouetted against the lowest level of the Ring: the shafts of the Mutine Mandala.

The Yanfolk prefer to keep a hill or two between themselves and such enigmas; therefore they gladly gave us this stretch of ground to site our homes, from the crest of my rise to the far side of the valley. Once I thought: how wonderful to see that splendid monument to vanished greatness every morning with the new light striking it, fired every noontide by the famous Flash! Now, though . . .

"Pompy!" he said, irritated. The chubble, half asleep, had rolled over and licked his bare toes with her long bluish tongue. But he was, in fact, relieved that he had been distracted from staring at the Mandala, the nearest and probably the most impressive of the incredible relics scattered as randomly as confetti over the face of Yan—randomly by the principles of mankind, at any rate, though perhaps not in the opinion of their builders.

He dropped into a chair which faced neither the river and the city nor the coloured translucent roofs of the Earthsiders' homes, darkening one by one in an irregular pattern as the occupants decided it was bedtime, but square towards the Northern Range. There the luminance of the Ring was caught by a patch of ice on the flank of Mount Fley, like a white jewel among the piled black hair of a queen. That was where, among eternal snows, the River Smor took its rise, the weeping of a glacier, as the Yanfolk said.

They did weep. And that was not the most extraordinary of their resemblances to mankind.

To his left and right lay the habitable lands: the fertile plains of Rhee cross-hatched with fields and orchards whose pattern had not altered in millennia, the pleasant rolling downlands of Hom dotted with thickets of nut-trees and traversed by herds of shy creatures like deer with long thick silver-grey tails, and the sloping plateau of Blaw where plants corresponding to fungi grew in fat succulent slabs from time-cracked rocks. The Yanfolk collected and dried their spores to make a coffee-like drink named morning-brew.

At his back, and to the south, was Kralgak, or as one might say "Dangerland"—that zone marked at night by stabbing white lances, on which the Ring continually hurled portions of its substance deflected from orbit by the neverceasing clashes between its particles. That was a fearful region, pocked like the skin of a loathsomely diseased face, into which neither humans nor Yanfolk dared venture for fear of being smashed by heavenly hammers. Southward again, in the corresponding subtropical zone, were the lands of the wilders, cousins of the northern Yanfolk but degenerate; their language had pared down to a few crude syllables and their only tools were sticks to grub for roots.

And beneath his feet, at the antipodes of Prell, was the water-hemisphere: the Ocean of Scand. There too, under the equatorial girdle of the Ring, the débris of the skies came slamming down and made the waves boil.

It was best not to think of Kralgak or the wilders at night, which was why all the houses of the Earthsiders' enclave standing high enough on the hillside to afford a view in that direction were arranged like Dr Lem's— with their main outlook to the north. Trying not to remember what it had cost this planet to enjoy the lovely shining arch spanning its sky, he gazed up towards the few stars which shimmered through the blurring dust of the stratosphere, like single raindrops caught on fur. Each was surrounded by a tiny rainbow halo, miniatures of the one which framed the sun by day in a polychrome haze less predictable than a kaleidoscope.

Why did I decide to come here?

The question sprang from his subconscious and took him by surprise. He had been asked it, often and often, because almost every year strangers—typically very young—wandered across the go-board to Yan looking for goodness knew what . . . and, with increasing frequency, it was Dr Lem among all the long-term residents that these birds of passage wanted to talk to. It was a curious sensation to be—well-known? Not exactly. Notorious? That wasn't the word, either. But, anyhow: to have been heard of, elsewhere in the galaxy.

The visitors always took to Pompy, and overfed her disgracefully.

Hmm! Where was I? Oh, yes.

There were convincing superficial reasons for his decision to settle on Yan. He could say, honestly enough, that he had almost reached the limit of his opportunities to travel; it was a strain on both body and mind to use the go-board, and he had begun his voyaging too late to acquire the adaptive flexibility some people rejoiced in. He had already been middle-aged. Moreover he was no longer so mentally resilient that he enjoyed coping with the crazy-seeming shifts of life-style found on planets wholly dominated by humans, which could oblige the population to change centuries overnight . . . so to speak.

He had therefore been looking for something stable—something, however, which would offer more than simply a chance to reflect and vegetate. The placid, quasi-pastoral existence of Yan would have appealed to him anyhow, he admitted. As a sort of bonus, though, it was shot through and through with enigmas which better minds than his had chip-chip-chipped at for almost a century. One could at least hope, he had said in a self-deprecating tone to so many of those youthful visitors, that constant exposure to them might help towards an eventual solution. And they would nod, distantly aware of the mystery of the wats and mandalas and menhirs dotted around the planet, all far beyond the capacities of modern Yanfolk and some—like the Mullom Wat—even exceeding the abilities of mankind.

So here he had been for thirty-odd years, wrestling with the riddle of *shrimashey* . . . and hunting desperately for meaningful equivalents to those Yannish concepts which performed the same function in linguistic terms as "science", "technology", "natural law", but which absolutely and incontestably could *not* be translated by those words . . . and, of course, butting his head against that conundrum above all which the Yanfolk posed: the question of how a species so astonishingly like mankind, equally intelligent, equally varied as regards temperament, could have done what they seemed to have managed millennia ago—decided that there was a *proper* way to live, and adhered to it for thousands of years with no discernible alterations.

Now and then he had fancied himself within grasping

distance of a key to all these problems together, as though he had been rattling the pieces of a jigsaw-puzzle back and forth in a box for years on end, and suddenly glanced down to see . . . Well, not the complete pattern, but enough to indicate how the remaining pieces should be added.

And somehow, every time, he had found he was wrong.

Yet he had never really hoped that that achievement would crown the time he had spent on Yan. He knew that.

No, in the last analysis I came here because . . .

Because Yan was at once a beautiful and a terrible world, everything about it seeming fined down to the barest essentials. Its range of contrasts, from the horrors of Kralgak to the idyllic paradise of Hom, was as great as might be found on any habitable planet; yet there was a grand simplicity about it. Each element composing the overall variety was unique: there was *one* great ocean, *one* harsh desert, *one* delightful garden-like prairie . . .

I felt—drawn.

The other meaning of that term provoked him to raise his fingertips and pass them across his face, knowing what a mirror would have shown him. Beneath his shock of grizzled hair his forehead was furrowed, while his cheeks were shrunken and his neck-tendons stood out like stretched cords. Under his gown the mildness of the spring night turned to the stone chill of approaching age.

I've grown old, Dr Lem admitted to himself. *I ought to start thinking about where I want to die. Here? But it's one thing to pick a planet to live on; to die on it is something else.*

When his thoughts took this morbid a turn, he realised, it was high time to put himself to sleep. He half-turned in his chair, stretching out a hand to prod

Pompy, and froze in mid-motion. Over the distant silhouette of the Mutine Mandala the white disc of the
moon was rising.

But there was no moon on Yan, and had not been
for nearly ten thousand years.

II

WHEN THE IMPOSSIBLE moon rose, Marc Simon was trudging gloomily homeward from what should have been a soirée at Goydel's house, a few paces behind his Yannish mistress Shyalee who was completely out of patience with him.

Tonight he had wound himself up to a climactic step, the most important since his decision four years ago to quit the Earthside enclave and settle in the upstream quarter of Prell among the artists, minstrels and fine artificers. Acquiring Shyalee had been as nothing compared to the simple act of moving to a small house with three rooms and a pool full of nenuphars; it had seemed like the natural extension of a single process.

Continued too long? After all, among the Yanfolk a woman never lived with a man for more than a year at a time . . . He was tempted for an instant to think that a change might cure his trouble. Then, catching sight of Shyalee ahead of him on the slanting street as she passed in and out of the gleam of a gloglobe over a house-door—boy-slim, heart-stoppingly beautiful—he knew it was only his current mood of frustration that had made him consider dismissing her. There would be

9

plenty of others willing to take her place. But the likelihood of finding somebody pleasanter to live with would be nil.

Although . . .

Briefly, he found himself wondering what it would be like to make love again with a girl having breasts and a skin all of one colour, who needed sometimes to break off from a kiss because she had to breathe in through her mouth. But that had nothing to do with his problem. Nothing at all. It was irrelevant.

Moreover he'd had the chance, now and then, and ignored it.

No, what I'm concerned about is—

Well, if only Shyalee had been able to understand what it had cost him to decide that tonight, at Goydel's soirée, he would move on from the translations in which he had so long specialised, and whose raw material he knew to be good because it was borrowed from talents greater than his own, to the presentation of an original composition in Yannish.

And then to find *shrimashey* in progress, the whole company lost in that mindless weaving pseudo-dance, forcibly regressed who could tell how many steps down the evolutionary ladder . . . !

Perhaps it had saved him from hideous embarrassment. Perhaps what he had proposed to offer his friends was no more than crude doggerel. Most likely he would have had no way of telling. The Yanfolk were always polite, and they were particularly polite to poets. When it came to an Earthsider poet, the politeness was redoubled; while the older Yanfolk did not share the unquestioning adulation which had turned so many of their young people into what the Earthsiders insultingly called "apes"—imitating Earthside clothing, manners and habits, salting their speech with human words— Earth and all things Earthly enjoyed indescribable cachet everywhere on this planet. So even the lousiest rubbish would have been assured of a warm reception.

And it would have been useless asking Shyalee's opinion in advance. She was fantastically beautiful, having delicate bones, huge dark eyes, slender limbs like wands, and of course that organ, the *caverna veneris,* which made its counterpart in a human girl seem like a spur-of-the-moment mechanical imitation. He had sometimes thought of it as being independently alive, and that was almost true, for it was controlled from that specialised ganglion near the base of the spine.

But he had had to argue and argue with her, before they left for Goydel's, to make her put on his favourite among her costumes, a webweave cloak of misty blue, finer than gossamer. She herself had wanted to wear Earthside dress—adapted by being slit under the arms, naturally, so that there was a free flow of air to her spiracles. She would never have become his mistress had she not practically worshipped Earth and Earthmen. Deaf to the grandeur of the Mutine Epics, scorning their subject as stale and of interest only to reactionary oldsters, she had long ago resigned herself to putting up with Marc's interest in Yannish poetry as one of the penalties she had to pay for being envied by her own generation of Yanfolk.

Paradox, Marc thought. *I could never have enjoyed Shyalee without that fault in her which I most detest!*

He had been so furious—so grief-stricken—when he found *shrimashey* at Goydel's, he had caught up one of the bowls of the *sheyashrim* drug and fully intended to gulp it down . . . even though he knew it didn't have the same effect on humans as on Yanfolk, didn't turn over the control of the body to the lower ganglion, but merely wiped out the cortex for a while, making the limbs twitch randomly and releasing the sphincters. It would have been a symbolic act. Only she had knocked the bowl out of his hand and told him, in detail, what a fool he was.

Right. I could have been staggering shamefacedly back this way, reeking of the content of my bowel.

Only . . .

Here was a question which Marc ordinarily avoided, but tonight could not. Had she saved him from his own stupidity for his personal sake, or merely because he was that walking wonder of the world, an Earthman?

He pictured himself as though he had been able to float out of his body and roost on the eaves of the house he was passing, to watch go by this lean, almost gaunt young man, his black hair and swarthy skin testifying to the intrusion of North Africans among the French who had bequeathed him both his name and his taste for patterns of words so strained and disciplined that one could hear them cry out under the concentrated load of meaning focused into every syllable. He could have been wearing Earth-style shirt and breechlets, but was not; having chosen to make his home among the Yanfolk, he had adopted their garb, the toga-like *heyk* and *welwa* cape.

Externals, to his lasting regret, marked the limit of his assimilation. He had to go back to the enclave now and then, though he kept his visits to a minimum. He could breathe Yannish air, drink Yannish water, take a Yannish mistress whose loveliness gripped his throat every time he looked at her—but this was not an Earthsider's world, made over to fit his race, and he sometimes had to step out of it, to buy essential foods or medicines, and endure the cold-shouldering, the scornful stares, the whispering behind his back . . .

It wasn't only his living with Shyalee which so angered the inhabitants of the enclave, he was sure of that. They treated Alice Ming civilly enough, and her situation was like this, although the sexes were reversed. She, however, was always among the first to dial the library when a new batch of Earthside tapes was delivered, and collected groups of apes to watch them with her lover. His name was Rayvor, but he preferred to be known as Harry.

Demonstrating the proper status of her species, Marc summarised sourly. *Whereas I've "gone native". I'm a traitor.*

What, though, was the point of being on a planet with intelligent aliens, unless one got to close quarters and tried one's hardest to understand? And that meant more than just a tumble with a native bed-mate now and then . . . an experiment he was sure almost every adult in the enclave must have tried by now, with the possible exception of old Dr Lem. Even that arrogant slob Warden Chevsky! And he actually boasted of not speaking a word of Yannish!

Doesn't it matter to them that the Mutine Mandala was standing tall and fine before the crudities of Stonehenge or the Pyramids were cobbled together by barbarians?

Presumably not. Yet this above all was what fascinated him about his adopted home: the sense that something wonderful had been accomplished, with a kind of finality about it, leaving behind the indelible impression that the Yanfolk were—were fulfilled. He had struggled often and often to convey to Shyalee and her friends his view of the relative merits of what Earthsiders and Yanfolk had done, trying to make them see why the blind random hunting which had carried humanity out among the stars was *not* automatically superior, because it could never lead to a satisfying conclusion. How could anyone foresee an end to the wanderings of mankind? Like the purposeless sprawl of a climbing plant humans had crept out from sun to sun, with no promise of an ultimate achievement to crown the scheme, such as he was sure he sensed on Yan. He believed beyond the possibility of contradiction that here some colossal task—logically the one described in the eleven books of the Mutine Epics—had been conceived, and undertaken, and concluded. Now, their struggles behind them, the Yanfolk were at peace.

Shyalee would not even listen to that kind of talk any longer. Nor would her friends. One could hardly say they had rebelled, because no members of the older generation had ever put more substantial obstacles in their path than an occasional caustic comment, but they had turned their backs on their own way of life. They thought everything Earthly was marvellous, preferring syntholon to webweave, alien tapes to their own infinitely subtle traditional culture-forms. Instead of accompanying him to Goydel's soirées, which he regarded as a tremendous honour because notoriously Goydel was the current arbiter of taste in Prell, he knew she would far rather have gone to Alice Ming's, sipped distasteful Earthside liquors with feigned enjoyment, gabbled the evening away in small-talk, as much in the foreign tongue as in her own.

Yes. She puts up with me. That's all our relationship amounts to.

Despair darkened his mind for a moment. Then, suddenly, he realised that—as though repenting of her short-tempered behaviour when they left Goydel's— Shyalee had stopped by the door of their home and was waiting for him. He hurried the last few yards and caught her hand, forcing a smile as he opened the door for her. It was not locked. Theft and burglary were contrary to Yannish custom, which meant they were literally unthinkable.

Together they stepped over the threshold into the atrium, where at the far end of an oval pool a fountain pumped ceaselessly among nenuphar-leaves. There was something a little Roman and something a little Japanese about this commonplace Yannish house where he had settled; instead of interior walls it had screens which could be moved aside in warm weather so that the paved centre court became an extension of the three small plain rooms with their sparse furniture and perfectly proportioned ornaments. The fountain had been an idea of his own, which had been copied widely by Shyalee's friends. As he had realised later, it was too vigorous to accord with authentic Yannish attitudes, because it repeated over and over the same unaltering pattern, wasting effort to an utterly predictable end. But before he recognised how out of keeping it was Shyalee had become too attached to it for him to have it removed.

"Do you want," Shyalee said, beginning in her own tongue and ending in his, "a nightcap?"

Rage gripped him for an instant: *how often must I tell you that I hate this ape's habit of mixing Yannish and human words?* But he restrained himself, and managed to nod, even though speech was for the moment beyond him. She vanished into the house, and he continued to his favourite stone seat overlooking the pond. As he went, he tugged from his baldric-slung pouch his copy of Book Nine of the Mutine Epics; currently he was revising his translation of it, and had taken it to Goydel's tonight just in case his original . . .

No, what's the use of fooling myself? Not "in case my original poem was so well received they asked for more." In case my courage failed me at the last moment . . .

Staring at the nenuphars, noting how the spring warmth had brough the buds forward, he murmured under his breath a snatch of the passage he was having most trouble with.

"By water standing fast, forging decision,
  Mastering fluid-flow, murky creation
  Carving a softness—"

He broke off. It wouldn't do. It simply would not *do*. It was lame, like a spavined horse driven under too heavy a load. The notion of "carving softness" lacked the paradoxical quality of the original, because carving suggested knives or chisels, hard sharp edges, whereas the root associations of the Yannish words implied that

the tool was softer than the material being worked—
like water eroding a rock. Yet "eroding" had overtones
of long patient geological processes, while the Yannish
verse made it clear that what happened took place instantly!

"Oh, hell," he said aloud. Was there any point in
going on? Was there any point in trying to sort out the
hard core of historicity in these baffling Epics? It went
without saying that behind these actual solid memen-
toes, the menhirs, the mandalas, the wats, behind these
fanciful descriptions of sunken continents and shattered
moons, there must lie objective truth. But how far towards which end of the scale?

The orthodox view was the rational one; about ten
thousand years ago, it declared, there had been a catastrophe—perhaps Yan's moon had been dragged from
orbit by the intrusion into this system of another body
of comparable size, or possibly there had been a collision. The moon had been barely outside the local
Roche's Limit. The event had either smashed it into
fragments, or else tugged it close enough to the planet
for it to pull itself apart. Either way, it had thereupon
become the Ring.

This fantastic calamity, according to the rational explanation, had shattered not only the moon but the
confidence of the Yanfolk. From a vaulting, ambitious
people with considerable scientific knowledge, they had
declined into a beaten one, half of whose world was
inaccessible to them thanks to the rain of meteorites
from the Ring, and most of whose technical achievements had been left to go to ruin while they contented
themselves with staying alive.

To console themselves for their retreat to a semi-
primitive existence, to excuse their decadence, they invented a myth about a vanished Golden Age which it
was futile to try and imitate because the greatest and
most powerful individuals of the species, the geniuses—

half poets, half scientists—whom humans referred to as "dramaturges", had been destroyed.

But according to that myth the dramaturges themselves had caused the breakup of the moon. In some sense, possibly this might be true. Some dangerous experiment—unlikely to have been the release of fusion-energy because Yannish "science" had taken a different route, but perhaps interference with molecular binding-forces—could have torn the satellite apart.

Yet no one had been able to determine whether the suspicion was correct. For Earthsiders there was a body of knowledge called "science", which began with steel and steam-engines and continued to go-boards and interstellar ships, but was a continuum at every stage, conditioned by an attitude of mind. If this system got results, the Yanfolk let it be inferred, in their opinion it was in spite of and not because of its postulates: a kind of magic. An Earthsider might argue that his view was correct because his machines worked when you switched them on. A Yannish opponent—not that they descended to this kind of debate—might quote Book Seven of the Mutine Epics and point to the Ring as evidence that that was also "the truth".

The proof of the pudding . . .

He heard a footfall behind him—Shyalee's. Reflexively he turned, expecting to take a cup from her, and found her staring foolishly into the sky. He copied her, and saw the moon.

III

OF THOSE INHABITANTS of Prell who had been asleep when the moon appeared, almost the first to be awakened were Speaker Kaydad and his present matron . . . to use the conventional term for a Yannish female keeping company with a householding male whose child she had not borne. (But the analysis of Yannish family relationships was complex.)

Their son and daughter—respectively, hers and his—had been among the group of seventeen young people who had passed the evening with Alice Ming and Rayvor. It was their shouts from outside which roused the household.

And seventeen loud voices on the street, dispersed over an area of several square kilometres, were quite enough to waken the entire population by a sort of chain-reaction. As those who had seen the moon alerted those who had not, gloglobes came back to life within half an hour of being extinguished, so that the town bloomed like a field of fantastic flowers: blue, red, yellow, green, white. In the enclave the communet buzzed frantically, all the rarely-used emergency circuits coming alive, as the inhabitants woke their friends or applied for explanations from the informat. Human and Yannish, clad and naked, people came out of doors to stare in amazement, abandoning dreams, the watching of tapes, music or making love. Shortly even babes in arms, seized by their parents and carried along for fear something might happen while a wall separated them, were lit by the strangeness in the sky.

"Your tireless efforts have, then, been rewarded," Speaker Kaydad's matron said to him in the mode of extreme respect reserved for persons of outstanding individual worth. But he replied in the mode of determined contradiction.

"No. Observe and analyse. That is no moon."

He could not disguise his fury and disappointment.

Indeed, it had become clear within a few seconds of the thing's appearance—at least to those who had bothered to learn about such matters—that this could not be a large heavenly body at a considerable distance. It moved far too fast, and must therefore be close, orbiting well inside the Ring. Even so, it was colossal; no artificial object of such apparent size had been seen in the vicinity of Yan before, unless perhaps in the days ten thousand years before when . . .

The idea stopped there, for most of the watchers.

Having regained his presence of mind, Dr Lem let go the grooved wooden rail of his verandah, at which he had had to clutch to steady himself. Something nuzzled his left leg. Thinking it was Pompy, he said aloud, "Easy, old girl—it's all right!" And reached down to pet her head.

Only his fingers encountered smooth chilly metal, and he realised in annoyance that the house's built-in medical reflexes had dispatched support mechanisms to him. Pompy was still asleep, her elegant whiskers trembling as she breathed.

He pushed the machines aside vigorously enough for them to get the hint, drew a deep breath, and resorted

to an ancient yardstick to try and determine the objects's angular diameter. Holding his thumb up at the
full stretch of his arm, he covered the disc with the nail,
and found the latter approximately twice as broad. In
other words, the thing subtended about a quarter of a
degree. However, being so much brighter than the Ring
under which it flew, it seemed larger, and no doubt de-
ceitful memory would later make people swear that it
had covered an eighth or more of the sky.

In its wake, as the Ring shed meteors, this too shed
tokens of its presence.

They began in the far north, where—as on any similar world—the local sun had stung the molecules of the
upper air into activity. Owing to the constant downward
shifting of particles from the Ring, there were always
vivid aurorae on Yan regardless of the season.

Now, as though a supernal finger had beckoned them
equatorwards, the potential gradients of the polar stratosphere stretched into long easy declines down which
poured the brilliant discharges of the arctic night. Huge
draping curtains of luminosity shook out their folds
along the course of the River Smor, bluish and yellowish and occasionally shifting without warning into deep
red. Free radicals sown from above sparked fresh reactions, so that the curtains seemed to draw apart, looping
upwards and becoming vast double inverted rainbows
with the colours interchanged. On the airy stage for
which the aurora now formed a sort of proscenium
arch, magnificent pyrotechnics began. Intangible jewels
glittered, fiery wheels resolved, blasts of lightning
threaded whiter than the eye could bear down the
black-with-silver background of the night.

After this phase came another which was totally abstract: a series of elegant swooping curves of colour and
light, as though some skilled master of an organ utter-
ing visual rather than auditory music had briefly chosen
to explore the harmonic relations between the notes of
a trivial theme given to him by a wealthy patron, before

attempting to make a more formal structure out of them. Following this sequence, which lasted ten or twelve minutes, there was a new series, a group of signs and portents. A huge fire-breathing monster stirred and spat flame and eventually swallowed its own tail. Next, two armed figures with swords and shields clashed in mid-heaven and dissolved into a flower with blue leaves and a white crown. Finally the entire sky was overspread by a brilliant yellow wheel, which rotated, fading, on its invisible axle and seemed to draw the dark in from its edges as it turned.

Terrified, her almond eyes so wide their slant was lost, her sallow complexion paled to stark ghost-white by her alarm, careless of the fact that she was bare to the waist on the balcony outside her dormicle and that to any of the Earthsiders gathered in the street who happened to glance this way her drooping breasts would not be an exotic marvel as they were to Rayvor-Harry, Alice Ming clutched at her lover's arm.

"What—what is it?" she whimpered.

Still in the Earth-style clothes he had worn during the visit of the seventeen youthful apes who had spent the evening here, he swallowed hard and tried to think of a reply which would not disappoint her. And could not.

He forced out finally, "I don't know!" The words emerged in Yannish, his grasp of human language destroyed by the shock of what he was saying.

"But your legends! Your ancient tales—your folklore!" Alice was eager to speak; if she didn't, her teeth chattered and the muscles of her jaw vibrated like a plucked fiddlestring. "Don't they tell about the time when your planet had a moon?"

Valiantly, Rayvor-Harry said, "That's all mythical nonsense. You told me so, lots of times."

But that was as far as his self-control extended. From that final declaration of scepticism he slid without intention into reciting a traditional Yannish formula of intercession, not addressed to any god—the Yanfolk, if they had ever worshipped supernatural beings, had long forgotten them—but invoking powers beyond knowledge, beyond science, beyond belief.

Also one witness was Vetcho, who held what was not an office, nor a rank, among the Yanfolk of Prell—because the very notion of authority was foreign to Yannish minds—but who behaved in such a manner that, so far as relations with the Earthsiders were concerned, it amounted to the same thing.

His first response was dual, and in real time at that: a facility largely due to his anatomy. With part of him he was thinking as Speaker Kaydad's matron had thought, that this was success after so much trouble. With the rest of him, he was wondering in a hurt tone of mind why the climactic step had been taken without his assistance.

Then the truth dawned. After which: as near as Yanfolk could come to objurgation, or cursing.

More or less, and much less than more, he thought: *Those devils, those fiends! There will be nothing left for us. Must they strip us even of the shadow of the echo of our pride?*

But he was resolved that they should not, even though they were adding this latest mockery to the long toll of insults so far recorded: that they dwelt in plain view of the Mutine Flash, that they set their automatics on the border of the go-board to prevent Yanfolk traveling to other worlds, that they pried into the mystery of the Epics, that they . . .

His matron emerged to join him at that point, and he was un-Yannishly rude to her. And said nothing about the moon not being a moon. Let her find out.

Warden Chevsky was asleep and snoring. Drunk. His wife Sidonie was awake at his side, having tried several times to turn him over so that his mouth would not fall open. The last time he had struck out at her in his sleep and she was now nursing what felt as though it would be visible as a bruise in the morning.

It was not her first failure of the night. She had tried to encourage him to make love when they came to bed, and been rebuffed. Now she sat up against the pillows, moodily hating him.

Is the bastard past it? Or has he acquired a mistress? A Yannish mistress? Would one of those delicate, fragile creatures look twice at him?

For a second or two the imagined spectacle of her husband's gross body conjoined with a Yannish girl made her want to laugh; it was so ridiculous. But the amusement faded quickly. She knew the answer only too well, and it was *yes.* The customs of the natives were—different.

So maybe I ought to do the same.

Short of celibacy, what was the alternative? No one in the enclave, no human male, would consider an affair with her, she was sure. It wasn't just that she was sixty-five and losing her figure; far more important, she was the wife of the Warden.

But one of these young Yanfolk, one of these "apes": he'd see me as a prize. Something exotic, wonderful. And Alice does claim that the Yannish anatomy—

A flash, a gleam, a whole blazing glory of light at the skylight window! She exclaimed and jolted her head up, blinking in disbelief. Her husband went on snoring.

She touched the skylight control and the panes slid back, showing her the sky direct.

Why, that can only be—! Back on Tamar, all those years ago, I remember . . .

No. More likely one of his imitators. But in any case this was an event. She jumped from the bed in high excitement, a cry rising to her lips, meaning to wake her husband even if it involved the risk of being hit again.

And checked the impulse.

No. Let the liquor-sodden swine be the last to find out. Maybe it'll lead to the loss of his job. I wouldn't weep.

As silently as possible she stole from the room, catching up a gown and stabbing her toes into slippers, and went out on the balcony to enjoy the play of colours while it lasted.

"Pompy, *shut up*," Dr Lem said in the tone he reserved for occasions when he really meant it. The chubble had been complaining because her sense of the fitness of things had been disturbed; this was not the time at which one sat down to the communet. Hurt, but resigned, she let her whiskers dangle dejectedly and folded herself into the sort of small package he recalled from the days when she was a mere kit and he was training her to behave in a human home, a variation of the ostrich principle: *if I can't see you you can't see me.*

"Hah!" Dr Lem said, wishing it were really that simple. He would have liked this thing in the sky to go away. Very much.

He had suddenly been overwhelmed by a sense of unwanted responsibility. He held no official post in the enclave—indeed, there was only one official post, Chevsky's—but with the passage of time he had become its doyen, and in consequence people tended to look up to him. Moreover, he had the cachet of his profession. Even a small community like this posed problems which now and then drove someone to seek psychiatric help, and he helped as best he could in such cases.

And he felt there were certain individuals who ought at least to realise, as soon as possible, what had happened. His colleague Harriet Pokorod, to start with, the community's medical doctor; Jack and Toshi Shigaraku, joint tutors-in-chief of the little school—there were not very many children here, either because people were understandably reluctant to start a family on a strange planet, or because the habit-patterns of the Yanfolk had affected them, but their position was clearly one of influence; Pedro Phillips, the merchant; Hector Ducci, responsible for everything technical in the enclave and above all for the maintenance of the go-board . . .

All of whom, apparently, were already talking on the communet. At least he was getting the busy signal whichever of them he tried to call.

Warden Chevsky? No, of course not. He's bound to have been the first one notified, and he must have his hands full.

Frustrated, Dr Lem leaned back in his chair. He wanted—needed—to *do* something, even if it was only talk to a friend. Or to the informat, he added, sullenly realizing that so far he was going on guesswork and second-hand data. He punched the informat code with trembling fingers, and in a moment discovered not only that he was correct in his conclusions, but that thirty-eight earlier inquirers had beaten him to them.

"What *is* it?" Shyalee whispered at last, having gripped Marc's arm so long and so hard that she had almost cut off the circulation with her fingers.

"It's—well, it's an advertisement," Marc said gruffly. He used the nearest available Yannish word. It meant much more than its literal human counterpart, but in this particular case it was not in the least an exaggeration.

"An advertisement!" Shyalee cried. "But that's absurd! What's it supposed to advertise?"

"The arrival of . . ." Marc hesitated, wiping his

forehead with the hem of his cape. "Well!" he said at length. "Have you ever heard any of us talk about a man called Gregory Chart?"

Eyes wide, mouth wide, she shook her head. That convention had been adopted at the time of the first human contact with Yan, and become a permanent part of the native repertoire of gestures.

"You will," Marc sighed. "No doubt of that."

IV

VIRTUALLY THE ONLY people in Prell and its vicinity who slept that night were infants, who crowed their appreciation of the pretty lights in the sky and relaxed happily in their mothers' arms, and the very old, who drowsed off while muttering dire warnings about celestial signs.

The Yanfolk were not personally but racially acquainted with such matters, and were kept awake by arguments between conservative factions who quoted mysterious passages from the Mutine Epics and other inscrutable sources, and opposing—mostly younger—schools of thought who maintained that here was another admirable manifestation of the superior human culture, this use of the entire welkin as a poster hoarding. It had not taken long for the information Marc had given Shyalee to spread by word of mouth far beyond the circle of her close friends. Perhaps an hour.

But when fuller details followed the first bald summary the arguments abruptly took a different turn.

Three X down, Erik Svitra said to himself, and went blue across the go-board, then purple. He was getting tired, and the guide-sequence he had memorised under hypnosis felt as though it would never end. *One X diagonal, and pi to the e . . .*

The board had been singing in F major. Abruptly it hit him with a bucket of nonexistent ice-water and put a smooth steel floor under his feet. He was through.

And about time, Erik thought. If he'd known how long and tough this sequence was, he might have thought twice about making the direct trip to Yan without stopovers. Still, at least the expensive hypnotic instructions had brought him out where he wanted to be. He sat down his travel-pack with relief and stared from the board's edge toward the shining Ring he'd seen so many pictures of.

Abruptly he spotted something orbiting under it. A moon.

What the—?

He snatched the informat print-out from his pocket and checked it for the umpteenth time. No moon.

Hell, they've sent me to the wrong planet! I'll—I'll sue the bastards!

But tomorrow. He was exhausted. Right now he had to find a place to lodge. Gloomily he shouldered his pack and began to trudge down the hill.

The news, of course, had spread within minutes to all the Earthsiders, not only because so many people had punched the informat for an explanation, and got one, but also because several hadn't needed to: Mama Ducci had been on Ilium when Chart came calling, Sidonie Chevsky had been on Tamar, someone else had been on Cinula, someone else on Vail . . . Everybody wanted to stay up and talk about him, and did so until the fantasia overhead died with the advent of dawn.

Meantime, the one exception to the general rule, Warden Chevsky snored.

At sunrise the moon came down from heaven anyway. Dwindling as it descended and shed the space-distorting refractory effects employed to make it seem vast beyond the stratosphere, it was nonetheless still huge when it settled: a plain white globe five hundred metres high, under whose released mass the Plateau of Blaw shuddered like Atlas grown tired of holding up the sky.

Some people claimed that they could sense completion, or fulfilment, here on Yan. What Dr Lem sensed was weariness. The very landscape suggested it; since the dissolution of its moon into the Ring, the mountains had begun to lie down under their own weight, and it was as a result of this that the land-surface was confined to a single hemisphere. Even the shallow ocean which rolled over the other half of the globe seemed to be stirred as much by the continual bombardment of meteorites as by the sluggish solar tides.

Outside the polar circles there was still one range rugged and high enough to boast permanent snowcaps and glaciers, but only one, last testament to a vigorous mountain-building youth. Over all of Blaw and Hom there was no peak bigger than a hill, much weathered, easy to climb. Moreover Prell had not always been at the mouth of the Smor, but had taken over from seaward towns as they surrendered to the encroaching waters. Because they could not swim without elaborate respiratory aids, the Yanfolk seemed unwilling to struggle with the sea. Now one could lean over the side of a boat on a clear day, fifteen kilometres south of Prell, and peer down into the ruins of what had once been a port. When winter gales made the waves surge aside, the highest towers breached the surface like the worn yellow fangs of a sick old dog.

And this morning, this sunrise, as he sat at his communet and learned more and more relevant facts about the situation the enclave had been pitchforked into—each more dispiriting than the last—he felt fatigue on that same grand scale permeating his very bones. His

mind was alert, for he had taken anti-sleep drugs, but
no drug ever invented could fight such weariness as
could overwhelm a planet.

Vaguely, while he watched the spectacle in the sky,
Marc Simon had been aware of comings and goings. He
was on the flat roof of his home, where he and Shyalee
often slept, after the Yannish manner, during warm
weather. It afforded a superb vantage-point.

Calls had come from the street-door, at first soft, later shouted as it became clear that the entire neighbourhood had been aroused anyway. Shyalee had gone
to answer, and—so, Marc presumed—relayed what he
had told her to her friends, probably in garbled fashion.
He had ignored these distractions. He was hardly capable of coherent thinking, for he was torn between two
utterly opposed reactions.

On the one hand, it had been said of Gregory Chart
that he was the greatest creative artist of all time . . .
and there was some evident grain of truth in the claim,
inasmuch as no one in history had ever tackled such
themes on such a scale. Marc himself had never had a
chance to witness one of his performances; he had seen
some of the consequences, though, years later, which
were still being experienced on Hyrax.

Naturally, anyone would wish to be present during a
Chart performance. But if his work on Hyrax was a fair
sample, then the impact of his coming here, coming to
Yan . . . !

There was a footfall behind him. A gentle tap on his
shoulder. He shrugged it away like an annoying insect.

"Marc," Shyalee said, "it is Goydel who has called."

What? Marc jumped from the cushion on which he
had been squatting, Yannish-style. It had taken him a
month of practice to achieve that without sending his
legs to sleep. And it was true: emerging from the oval
opening at the head of the steps giving access to this
roof, he recognised the familiar features of his—well,

the nearest human term might be "patron", only there was no question of financial assistance involved, only of sponsorship and the granting of opportunities to present an artist's work to an appreciative and discerning audience.

Well, at least he wasn't the one who got killed during shrimashey, Marc thought . . . and realised that that was probably the unspoken fear which had so upset him a few hours ago, caused him to make that stupid gesture with the bowl of *sheyashrim* drug. But there was hardly a mark on Goydel, apart from a small patch of ointment on his forehead, where part of his crest of hair had been torn away.

Impossible to picture this staid, dignified personage in the middle of a heap of writhing, struggling bodies . . . Who did get killed, if anyone? A friend of mine?

But one must not ask. One was permitted to learn only by indirect, oblique routes. And sometimes all the participants survived, after all.

He strode forward, full of apologies that the old man should have had to negotiate the steep stairs. Goydel countered instantly, not in Yannish but in the Earthsiders' tongue, which he spoke with an excellent accent and a good command of idiom.

"No, young friend, I prefer to be up here, believe me. These remarkable displays overhead are not to be missed! Tell me, is it correct what I have been told, that this announces the arrival of one of your greatest human artists?"

Bustling around in a most un-Yannish manner, Marc was tugging up a cushion for him to sit on, whispering instructions to Shyalee about bringing a jug of morning-brew and some cakes, and generally fussing like a house-proud hostess caught unawares. He mastered all these impulses with an effort, steadied his breathing, and after making certain Goydel was comfortable squatted facing him and composed his limbs into a deliberately relaxed posture. The aurorae were almost over by now, but from them and the lightening east came plenty of light to see each other by.

There was a proper period of silence, terminated when Shyalee had produced the refreshments. Marc said diffidently in Yannish, "As to the personage responsible for the lights above us: yes, one might reasonably refer to him as an artist."

In his host's tongue again, from courtesy, Goydel said, "And what *sort* of an artist is he—this man Chart?"

"Why, he's . . ." Marc hesitated, and decided to fall in with Goydel's choice of language. Not that that made it much easier for him to explain.

How do you sum up Chart? In half a dozen sentences? You can't. Not in any language!

Still, he must do his best. He said after long reflection, "Well, first of all I should admit that I've never seen him work, but only talked with people who have. I understand that he's—he's an interpreter of dramas on a colossal scale. He tries to actualise a situation so that the people of a planet can live in it for as long as they can afford to pay him. It may be a dream, an ambition. Or it may be a period of past history. Or it may be a choice among a dozen possible courses of future action. I believe his range is enormous."

"It is the first time since the original visit of your species to our world that we have seen a spaceship. He invariably travels in that fashion, not by go-board?"

"Yes, I believe so." Marc licked his lips. He was always ill at ease when talking about interstellar travel with Yanfolk; so many of them envied human freedom to go from star to star, but there was an inflexible rule against nonhumans entering a go-board.

"Does he always announce his arrival the same way?"

"I heard that he did on Hyrax. First there was an extra moon in the sky—the moon of Hyrax is red, like old dry meat, and the new one was silvery, as you have seen. Afterwards there were auroral displays, though less elaborate and well-controlled. They showed me tapes."

Of course you'd expect him to refine his techniques over the years . . .

"And in the case you know of, what was the content of the performance?"

"Oh—on Hyrax it was a dream. Which turned sour." Marc grimaced. "About being happy under the rule of the Quain family. Don't ask me for all the details, please. I gather the rulers engaged Chart thinking that he would provide a circus for the people, to reconcile them to their condition, and expecting that afterwards their subjects would be happy to be ground just a little harder to meet his fee. His charges are not low.

"But the dream ended, and the reality took over, and the last I heard the people of Hyrax were still paying."

Goydel gave a nod. Marc realised that there were good reasons why Yanfolk should at once grasp the concepts underlying Chart's work. If there was any historical truth hidden in the obfuscation of Yannish traditional lore, it related to another event for which payment was still being exacted—after millennia.

"By what means does he achieve his effects?" Goydel inquired eventually.

Marc deliberately misunderstood the question. "Why, I believe basically it's a variant of the weather-control techniques employed on many planets, adjusting potential gradients within the natural layers of the atmosphere, then sowing patterns of activated molecules . . ."

His voice died away under Goydel's impassive level gaze, and he covered a momentary fit of embarrassment by sipping his own drink—coffee, because morning-brew contained an ascorbic-acid antagonist and an Earthsider who drank it developed scurvy.

"As to the way in which he involves whole planetary populations in his performances, though," he resumed, setting the cup aside, "there I'm afraid I know only the barest outlines. I know he starts by using gross techniques to adjust emotions—weather, again, is an example. Then he provides certain large-scale constructs which condition the reactions of people in their vicinity, either by their mere shape and colour or by subliminal emanations, and he sets the drama itself in motion with programmed volunteers, or androids. If there are mass media, he requisitions them. And I believe he may also use drugs, in drinking-water or air. But I don't imagine anyone fully understands his methods except himself."

"Is he, then, the only practitioner of his art?"

"I believe he has imitators. But none of them is regarded as his equal."

There was a further pause. Goydel said at last, reverting to Yannish, "It would not be wrong to suggest that you are unenthusiastic about this arrival?"

"It would not," Marc agreed, after unravelling the procession of negatives which decorated the formal hypothetical quasi-optative structure of the sentence. No modern human language could cram so many into so few words.

Next, he expected Goydel to ask him why not. The old man, however, did nothing of the kind. He merely drained his cup and rose.

"Must you go already?" Marc demanded, also standing up. He felt the need to go on talking, to bring into the open some of his misgivings, to try and explain why he was in two minds about Chart's visit. But Goydel, impeccably polite, rebuffed him expertly.

"Your hospitality has been most generous," he said. "At this contrary-to-custom hour for sociable intercourse, however, it would be unbecoming to trespass beyond the limit set by this unforeseen event . . . would it not?"

In Yannish terms at least: yes, it would.

V

THE DISCUSSIONS AND arguments flowed pro and con, while the featureless white globe rested on its bed of crushed rock, as though waiting for some giant to come along and roll it, tumbling, among the skittle-houses of Prell.

Exhausted, Erik Svitra had laid down his pack long before reaching the small town whose multicoloured lights he had clearly seen from the crest of the hill on which the go-board was sited. There was some sort of soft growth on the ground here—even by the light of the Ring and these curious aurorae, he couldn't make out details—and a bush overhung a cup-shaped depression, offering shelter. He had at first only meant to rest for a while; in the end, however, he had dozed off.

And was now waking to an itch.

He blinked his eyes open, and found that through a gap in the branches of the bush he had taken refuge under he could see the sun, a few degrees above the horizon, and encircled by just the sort of halo he had expected on Yan. But that had to take second place in his attention. Both his light-brown, plump legs were swelling up into a kind of magnified goose-flesh condition, and he had apparently been scratching himself in his sleep, because he had rubbed a small raw patch.

Oh, hell, he thought, and fumbled in his pack for an antidote. *Just my luck. Fresh off the board, and here I've been hit with an allergy already.*

He applied a thin film from a spray bottle, and was returning it to the pack when he heard footsteps. Cautious, he peered out between the branches, and saw someone coming towards him who was apparently suffering from a bad skin infection, dark patches on both . . .

He caught himself. He had been so tired when he came off the board, he'd convinced himself he was on the wrong planet after all. But if he wasn't, and the Ring, the halo around the sun, and now this—this person who obviously had proper Yannish skin-colouring, indicated that this must indeed be Yan, something very odd was going on.

A pace or two behind the Yannish . . . girl? Yes, girl, he deduced after consulting his informat printout again. A pace or two behind her, anyhow, a man followed, who had a regular human beard although he wore weird clothing. Erik rose into sight and hailed him.

"Say, friend!"

Both the man and his companion barely glanced his way.

"Say, I'm just off the board! Where can I find a hotel—and who do I report to?"

"Report?" the man echoed. His girl-friend was staring at Erik with a curiously searching expression. Of course, this was the planet where you could . . . But that would have to wait. He was looking forward to checking out the truth behind the rumours, though.

"Yes, report!" Erik scrambled up from the hollow where he had been sleeping, whipped by the branches of the bush—he saw now it had peculiar greyish flowers on it—and confronted them. "See, I'm a freelance drug-tester, and I decided I'd come here and check out this stuff they have, this shay . . . Whatever. So I guess I ought to report to someone, and find a place to lodge."

"They don't have hotels here," the man said curtly. "I don't know you have to report to anybody, either. But I guess if you really want to you could track down Warden Chevsky. Down there in the enclave." He waved vaguely back the way he had come. "Ask anybody where he lives—they'll direct you. Come on, Shyalee."

He caught the girl's hand and hurried her onward. Staring after them in dismay, wanting to shout out what he thought of their rudeness to a new arrival, Erik saw the monstrous looming bulk of the ship for the first time.

What in the *galaxy* . . . ?

He licked his lips nervously, glancing around. On the track from the town, he spotted more people coming this way. He could ask them. Shouldering his pack, he waited for them to pass.

What was that up ahead? Dr Lem snapped his fingers to try and make Pompy hurry—the chubble, who clearly felt she desrved a larger ration of sleep, was in a cantankerous mood and kept falling behind—and took advantage of the fact that there was a metre-high bank beside the path at this point to gain a better view. Surely it couldn't be a crowd! There simply were not crowds on this planet; assemblies of large numbers of people in one place at one time were contrary to Yannish custom, and there were only three hundred twenty-odd humans, many of them children.

But it was a crowd. And more and more people were hastening to join it.

He hadn't looked back since leaving his house. Now he did, and discovered that in his turn he was being followed, by Jack and Toshi Shigaraku and—apparently—the entire roster of pupils at the enclave's little school, in a straggling line. Many of them knew Pompy, and on sighting her came running over with cries of delight.

"What is going on?" Dr Lem demanded as Jack Shigaraku came in earshot.

The tutor gave a shrug. "Well, obviously it was pointless trying to run regular classes today. So I ran through the article 'Chart, Gregory' on the encyclopedia setting of the informat, and here we are on the way to an unscheduled open-air lesson."

Around him the children grinned broadly.

"Has anything happened?" Toshi asked. "I mean since the ship landed. We heard it was down."

Falling in beside them, Dr Lem shook his head. "No, I've been trying to reach Hector Ducci—he'd know about this kind of thing if anyone would. I don't believe a ship has put down here since the initial contact. And I also tried to talk to Chevsky. But no one's answering on his 'net."

"Probably out here already," Toshi said. "Everybody else seems to be."

Ahead, the cries and laughter of the children had attracted the attention of a number of Yanfolk, bound in the same direction, who gazed at them curiously. They did not educate their children in groups; instead, they transferred them—starting the day after birth—along an incredibly subtle network of relations, which might easily take them to a dozen cities or villages, to let them absorb gradually the "life-style" of their race. Commonly this process might be over by the age of forty— the Yanfolk were long-lived, and the whole tempo of their existence seemed to be slowed down to correspond. Speaker Kaydad, for example, was known to be nearly two hundred, Earth-years. Occasionally it ended sooner; Shyalee, Marc's mistress, was reputedly only thirty-four. Very rarely it lasted a great deal longer; Speaker Kaydad had a son, in addition to the daughter currently living with him and his matron for the year, and that young man had not become a householder until he was forty-seven.

No, Dr Lem thought. *Groups to them don't have anything to do with education. They signify something else entirely.*

He felt himself shiver, despite the warmth of the morning.

His fat dark face traversed by beetling brows and magnificently menacing mustachios, Hector Ducci swore to himself in his ancestral Italian. He was a big, heavyset man, but in spite of his weight he was active, and he had been the first to arrive here, near the spot where the ship had set down. He had thought it his responsibility; he was, after all, the go-board supervisor as well as being in charge of the enclave's technical facilities generally, and ships were so rare these days no routine existed to cope with them. But they presumably fell under the head of on-world arrivals when they landed. So here he was, and everyone else appeared to have followed him, to this last outcrop of the yellowish, stratified rock constituting the Plateau of Blaw. On foot, of course. It was the standard Yannish mode of travel; the Yanfolk themselves thought nothing of walking for a fortnight, dawn to dusk.

However, he had been here for well over an hour, and the ship had just sat there, featureless, doing nothing and ignoring the calls he addressed to it over his portable communet extension. He had studied it with binox, and he was none the wiser.

Where the hell had Warden Chevsky got to? This was his pigeon, surely! What was a Warden for, if not to deal with—with whatever this kind of thing was?

Crisis, he thought with glum satisfaction. *Yes, that's what it's bound to be.*

He raised his binox again and swept the entire field of view with them, noting—to his surprise—that there were now far more Yanfolk assembling at the edge of the ship's shadow than humans. It was humans who were supposed to be the insatiably curious species, the rubberneckers. When told about their degraded cousins in the southern hemisphere, the wilders, the Yanfolk had allegedly shown no surprise and very little interest, on the grounds that "something of the kind was to be expected".

Still, presumably most of these would be apes. He didn't know enough of them personally to be sure through binox.

On impulse, he turned clear around, meaning to look down towards Prell, and checked; he had glanced in the direction of the go-board, and it was active. A harsh blue haze surrounded it, and there was the characteristic teeth-jarring hum.

"Zepp!" he shouted, and his eldest son Guiseppe, eighteen, as yet slim but by his dark hair and heavy bones due to turn into a fair copy of his father one day, strolled out of a clot of people fifty metres away.

"What is it?" he called.

"Go see who that is coming off the board!"

"Must I? Is it so important?"

Binox levelled, Ducci waited to be able to answer; the haze was fading. And there was . . .

"Hell, yes! It's important!" he exclaimed. "That's the last thing we need right now! It must have been tipped off."

"What is it?" Guiseppe hurried up to him and seized the binox. "Oh, it's only a news-machine," he said after a pause. "What's wrong with that?"

"You'll find out," Ducci said grimly. He had his own premonitions of what was going to emerge from all this, and they weren't pretty. "Get over there and inactivate it."

"But that's illegal! They're allowed to go anywhere, if they don't invade privacy," Guiseppe pointed out.

"I don't mean wreck it," his father snapped. "Just delay it for a while." Retrieving the binox, he studied the thing's angular, glinting form, long legs tipped with climbing-hooks and suction-pads disposed around the self-powered motor unit and the cluster of extensible sensors. "Luckily it's one of the old marks, an Epsilon, not a recent one like a Kappa or Lambda. It'll take a while to orient itself. Go on—feed it a rumour or something, send it on a false trail. It's important!"

Scowling, Guiseppe moved away with no detectable enthusiasm.

Still no sign of life from the ship, Ducci discovered when he turned around again. But more and still more people were pouring up the track from the town, including the entire roster of schoolchildren under the leadership of their tutors, the Shigarakus, and . . . He had to check twice with the binox before he could convince himself. Lord! Wasn't that the Speaker himself, Kaydad, and Vetcho too, the man who acted as his deputy, or assistant? You'd expect to see all the young apes out here, but never in a million years the old, conservative, hard-liners like them! He'd tried to be friendly towards them when he first arrived, ten or eleven years ago, thinking that they'd be interested in Earthsider gadgetry even if only because of what it did. But they'd been so frigid and distant, he'd given up.

He wasn't normally an imaginative man. But there was something about this situation that made his scalp crawl.

Crazy place! Crazy people! Not for the first time, Erik Svitra wondered nervously whether he had really got over that stuff he'd discovered on Groseille, that *gifmak* drug that cross-connected the perceptual channels in the mind. It had been the one big success of his career, and staked him to this life as a freelance. But they'd had to cure him of it, of course. At least, they'd said they had. Finding himself here, in this weird situation, made him uncertain about that. Here were all these people, both human and native, getting out of town just to go look at that starship up there—big, sure, but . . .

"Hell, what's a starship?" Erik grumbled aloud. "Might as well go look at a steam locomotive! In fact that could be more fun, because they had things that like whizzed around all the time!"

Still, he appeared to have located his destination. He had been directed six or eight times so far, and part of his route had taken him through what he deduced must be the Yannish section of town, where small ovoidal structures with flattened, partly-enclosed roofs stood with their doors open and seemingly nobody at home; then over this rise—which made his pack feel abominably heavy, but the informat printout had warned him there were no moving pedways or rented antigrav trolleys here—and now down into the relatively familiar, reassuring environment of the so-called "enclave": houses that were practically hovels by the standards he was used to, having at most two storeys, but recognisably human-designed.

And this was the address he'd been given for Warden Chevsky. A house larger than the average, with a big balcony, and a regular Earth-style annunciator at the door. He hit the contact-plate and called Chevsky's name.

Shortly, he heard a yell from inside: "Sid! Damn you, go answer that!"

There being no sign of "Sid", Erik hit the plate again. More yelling. Then, on the balcony over the door, a gross man appeared, belting a robe about him, hair tousled, eyes red, squinting at the daylight as though he had a severe hangover. Erik judged, with his expert's eyes, that it was due to alcohol, not something decently exotic.

With a barely-concealed trace of contempt, he said, "Are you Warden Chevsky?"

"Hell, yes!" The man rubbed his eyes. "Where the hell is my wife? Where's—well, where's everybody?" he added, seeming to take in the completely empty street for the first time.

"Oh, they're all crazy," Erik shrugged. "Gone out of town to look at some damned starship or other. Now, look! I'm Erik Svitra, and I'm—"

"What starship?" Chevsky broke in.

"I don't know!" Erik snapped. He was getting annoyed with this planet. Then: "Oh, I guess I do," he admitted. It wouldn't be politic to get on bad terms, right at the start of his stay, with this character they called the Warden. Some places didn't look kindly on people in his profession.

"Yeah, someone did mention something—someone I asked directions of, coming here," he continued. "There was some sort of show in the sky, they said, and then this thing came down around dawn, and the owner's supposed to be . . . Cart? No: Chart. Or some such name."

For an instant Chevsky looked at him with such fury he flinched, expecting the man to hurl himself bodily over the balcony. Then he vanished inside, and slammed the windows.

"Hey!" Erik shouted. And then again: "Hey!"

There was no response.

"Well, shit!" he said at last, and hoisted his pack again and turned away at random. "Sooner I get off this crazy world, the better!"

Only how? Unless he made a strike here, perhaps with this stuff called *sheyashrim* that the natives were supposed to use, how could he afford to pay to have himself programmed with the hypnotically-ingrained directions for a go-board trip to some more promising planet?

"I wish I'd never come here," he told the warm spring air.

Besides, he was hungry, and his feet hurt.

VI

WHAT WOULD BE the best solution to all this? To appeal to Earth and have Chart's ship forcibly removed? That question throbbed in Dr Lem's mind as he toiled up the last few metres of incline to the plateau-edge from which a clear sight could be had of Chart's ship.

But he didn't have any authority to ask for that. He doubted if anyone did, except possibly Chevsky—and Chart carried a great deal of weight. He was famous! A galactic celebrity! Not the sort of person the ghostly, ineffectual grasp of Earthside government could pick up bodily from a distant planet and send on his way with a slapped backside!

Even if the idea proved feasible, the sight of a major police action—and shifting a ship that size by force was bound to be a major action—would doubtless open whole new vistas in the Yanfolk's conception of mankind. Ill-founded it might be, but the rather chilly respect the natives accorded these barely civilised creatures, humans, for the sake of their manifest material achievements was better than the available alternatives.

On the other hand, anything Chart did would entrain

consequences quite as devastating, and infinitely less predictable . . .

Well, some sort of crunch was probably inevitable. Life in the enclave was far from typical of most human planets, being quasi-pastoral, almost idyllic. Even that much contact, however, had produced a serious disruption in Yannish society. Those pitiable "apes"—he formed the term in his mind with distaste, although he knew it was at worst patronising, because hardly any of the inhabitants of the enclave could ever have seen a real ape—they were only the most conspicuous symptom.

The nub of the problem was there, though. When humans discovered Yan, they had at least had some data from previous encounters with non-human intelligence to guide them, Although no other star-flying races had been encountered, at least seven were known with whom it was possible to communicate fairly well. There was even a convincing theory to explain why these were all bipedal, bisexual and binocular.

Also there were non-humanoid creatures which were suspected of being intelligent in some private fashion . . . but only time, and long patient study, would show whether the suspicion was correct.

Granted, the Yanfolk had been comparatively lucky. Their incredibly close resemblance to humans had preserved them from being turned into exhibits, or laboratory specimens. What men had learned about some of the other races had been garnered by explorers sent out by—for example—the Quains, those despots whom Chart had overthrown on Hyrax, answerable to no one but themselves and their bosses, and was the result of kidnapping ("random sampling"), psychological torture ("stress response analysis"), and poisoning ("metabolic research").

But then, when it was discovered that humans and Yanfolk could make love . . .

Well, that was just one of the improbable facts to

conjure with. Additionally, they were highly peaceable. Yet they endured the depredations of *shrimashey,* commitment to a brutal, random, violent means of population-control! And if one sought to get to grips with the reason, one had to travel by way of such human concepts as "holy," "sacred," "taboo." Not what you would predict for a rational species.

Yet rational they certainly were—and intelligent, and self-aware. At some time in the past, as the wats, mandalas and menhirs demonstrated, they had been technically more advanced, in some fields, than mankind was now. But they appeared to have lost interest in that kind of thing. Their society had been stable for millennia. Custom ruled them, not governments, and they had no officials or administrators—just an informal clique of certain persons who were *hrath,* or "optimal": in other words, peculiarly able to convey the sense of "rightness" or "propriety" to the next generation.

Nonetheless, when the arrival of aliens from the stars posed a brand-new problem, they reacted promptly and with perfect aptness. They singled out one of their number and called him *Elgadrin:* "one-who-speaks-for".

And . . .

Dr Lem blinked in astonishment. He had separated from the tutors and their retinue of children, and was now looking around for someone he could share his forebodings with: Ducci, perhaps, or the merchant Pedro Phillips. But his gaze had landed instantly on the unmistakable features of Speaker Kaydad, accompanied by Vetcho, and both of them were starting in his direction, bowing politely.

He wanted to turn and run, but he couldn't. At his side Pompy—overjoyed by all the attention the children had lavished on her—crooned with contentment. He wished he could get so much simple pleasure out of life.

The Speaker himself was a trifle taller than the Yannish average, his height enhanced by his crest of blue-black hair, which fanned out over his crown from pointed ear to pointed ear and down his nape to the level of his armpits. Lack of the normal widow's-peak over each eye was almost the only token, apart from his slow gait and speech, by which one might have guessed his extreme age. He was, of course, scarred in several places, and two of his fingers had been broken and healed crooked, but that was the inevitable consequence of *shrimashey,* and could have happened to him at any time from sixty onward.

Like all his kind, he looked at a casual glance as though he wore a mask. His forehead, scalp and eye-ridges were pale, a light wooden colour between white and brown. Both his cheeks, however, were of a red shade like seasoned mahogany, and the whole of the rest of his skin was patched with palm-sized areas of the same hue networked with irregular lines of the lighter colour. There was a hypothesis to the effect that while humans had evolved among scrub and along seashores, Yanfolk were of glade stock, but there was no proof of this, Yanfolk being remarkably uninterested in their ancestry. It was a guess based on analogies with Earth-side creatures such as giraffe and zebra.

Apart from his pigmentation, he differed visually from a human male in having tufts of hair at knees and elbows, and if he had been nude one could have seen the genital proboscis which, in a sense, symbolised the whole series of difficulties radiating from this contact between species.

Of course, the deeper one went the more marked the differences became. His liver-kidney was at the front of his abdomen; his heart was in his pelvis; on either side of it, in front of the hip-joints, were the male rudiments of twin organs which in the female corresponded to breasts, nourishing the new-born infant with a clear serum from special glands adjacent to the intestine. And his lungs were at his sides, drawing air directly through spiracles between the ribs; like a bagpipes, they had continual throughput. Sound to talk with was generated by a tympanal membrane and relayed through resonating chambers in the gullet, giving a rather pleasant, if monotonous, timbre; in Kaydad's case, resembling a 'cello droning away on a single note.

Those superficialities apart, however, it never ceased to amaze Dr Lem just how closely their two species resembled one another. Limbs, spine, skull, eyes, mouth—the list of likenesses was far longer than the tale of contrasts. *Who cares,* Dr Lem always thought, *if they can talk for an hour without pausing for breath? Just so long as their brains shape concepts we can grasp!*

And then he glanced past the approaching Speaker and saw the inevitable band of apes trailing behind Alice Ming and her lover: determinedly imitating Earthly clothing, fidgeting to try and keep concealed the breathing-slits cut in their upper garments, somehow surrounded by the permanent aura of resentment which, he knew, was due to their not being allowed to visit other planets.

Perhaps, he thought now, *it isn't a good thing after all?*

But at least the glimpse of those apes had given him a clue to the reason why Kaydad was seeking him out, to talk to him.

Kaydad's notoriously a conservative type, not as chauvinistic as Vetcho or introverted as—what's his name?—Goydel, but a great respecter of the status quo. If someone has told the Yanfolk about Gregory Chart, I bet the youngsters are all for having him perform here, and I bet that's the last thing Kaydad's generation want: some arrogant Earthling meddling in their prized ancient lore!

Because that was the only thing which could have tempted Chart here. He was certain his deduction was right.

And this could lead to a satisfactory conclusion after all. Smiling, he greeted Kaydad with hand outstretched.

* * *

"Anything happened yet, papa?" Guiseppe Ducci panted as he hurried up to his father.

"Speaker Kaydad just cornered Doc Lem over there," Ducci grunted, binox still to his eyes as though they had become glued there. "And—"

"About the ship, I mean!" Guiseppe interrupted.

"No, nothing." And, suddenly remembering, Ducci rounded on him, at first forgetting to lower the binox, then peeling them away with a sucking noise. They had left big curved grooves on the upper edges of his cheeks.

"Did you fix the news-machine?" he demanded.

"Oh, sure!" Guiseppe laughed. "It's old, like you said. Sort of goofy. Too many trips across the go-board, maybe. It went into the usual routine—'What events of galactic note have occurred here . . . ?' All that crap. So I sent it down into Prell, using the major population centre circuit. It'll be tied up for hours trying to figure what disaster emptied the town."

"Good boy," Ducci said, clapping him on the shoulder.

"Morning, Hector—morning, Zepp," a worried-sounding voice said, and they turned to find Pedro Phillips, the enclave's merchant, approaching them. "Say, have we had any confirmation that that is Chart aboard the ship?"

He rubbed his hands together reflexively. He was almost a paradigm of the merchant type, a portly man, though not as stout as Ducci, with a too-ready smile and a keen mind.

"I've been trying to get acknowledgments out of him," Ducci said, hefting his communet extension. "So far, not a word."

"I see." Phillips frowned. "I'm beginning to wonder if it is Chart in there, you know. I mean, I can't see what would bring him here. Surely he doesn't imagine three hundred of us in the enclave can afford his rates?

And as for the Yanfolk hiring him—well, how'd *they* pay him?"

Ducci nodded. Yannish currency did exist, but it related to a complex and subtle system of personal obligations, not to what humans would call a financial transaction.

"I guess he could just have come to look the planet over," Guiseppe offered. "Like a visit."

"Not in a million years," Phillips declared, and Ducci nodded agreement, tugging at his mustachios and frowning dreadfully. No, it couldn't just be a visit. Startravel was not a cheap pastime, even for someone like Chart—if there was anybody like him—who signed contracts with continents and spoke as an equal with the governments of planets.

"Ever seen him working?" he asked Philips. The merchant shook his head.

"Can't say I want to, either."

"Oh, I do!" Guiseppe exclaimed. "Mama was on Ilium when he came—you know about that?" he added to Phillips in parenthesis. "And she says it was wonderful!"

"Well, it's not up to us, anyhow," his father said after a pause. "You saw that Doc Lem is over there talking to the Speaker? I bet I know what they're discussing. The apes might want Chart to put on a show here, but the old folk—hell, no!"

"I sure hope you're right," Phillips muttered.

Since his belly was even emptier than the houses, Erik Svitra had finally decided to take the risk of helping himself to some food. He'd found a locally-made bread, with a good flavour, and a wedge of something cheese-like, strong but edible. There was a mouthful of it on the way down when he heard a tapping at the door. He jumped, inhaled a crumb, coughed, blew a wet mixture of bread and cheese all over the table he was sitting at, and the world dissolved into a swirling blur as his eyes filled with tears.

"It's okay!" he forced out as soon as he could. "I was just hungry—I'll pay for what I . . ."

But his vision had cleared by that time, and he was able to make out the nature of the intruder: an elderly Epsilon news-machine, of a type he had often encountered while crossing the go-board.

"Well!" he said sourly. "I guess I'm the only news in town today, hm?"

The machine said, seeming agitated as it wove its sensors back and forth in a complex pattern, "Sir, since it would appear you are the sole survivor of the catastrophe which has emptied this town of its inhabitants *à la* the apocryphal ocean-going vessel, *Marie-Celeste*, kindly inform me if you can of the nature of the said event."

"Catastrophe?" Erik blinked rapidly several times. "What catastrophe? Everyone's gone out of town to look at a starship that landed. Belonging to"—he searched for the name again, located it—"Gregory Chart, I think they told me. Say, I—"

But the machine had reacted in the most extraordinary manner. It had withdrawn its sensors, stood trembling for a moment, and then spun around in its own length and departed at a headlong run.

"What a world," Erik sighed. "Drives even machines crazy!"

He went back to his bread and cheese.

VII

THE SHIP HAD lain inert for so long that hardly anybody now was paying it much attention. It came as a shock when without preamble a vastly amplified but pleasantly inflected voice suddenly rang out all around it.

"Good morning! This is Gregory Chart. Forgive me for having taken so long to confirm what you doubtless already suspected, but after a lengthy interstellar voyage there are certain essential routine procedures to attend to."

The haloed sun was well clear of the horizon by this time. Oddly, both humans and Yanfolk seemed to be approaching the ship no closer than the fringe of its blurred shadow. And they had not surrounded it on all sides, but predominantly on the side nearer Prell, forming a rough horseshoe. All the watchers now, without exception, turned to face the source of the words.

"I believe that—yes, there he is. A friend of a friend of mine is present, I discern, who happens also to be a prominent member of your community. While we are not, regrettably, yet in a position to mingle with you, we'd like to invite him aboard straight away. When Dr Yigael Lem has finished his current conversation . . . ?"

A section of the ship's hull slid back, or dissolved—it happened so quickly, the naked eye could not determine which. A pale grey access ramp licked out like the tongue of a chubble, to touch the irregular rocky ground. Down this ramp a vast mass of roses spilled, and a fanfare roared from a score of amplified trumpets. Some of the Yannish apes clapped their hands gleefully; that was another convention they had copied from Earthsiders.

Next, kicking the flowers aside with careless boots, appeared an honour guard of soldiers two metres tall, in black skin-hugging uniforms with high red shakos on their heads. They took station either side of the ramp, five deep, and at a barking word of command slammed their weapons into salute position. Drums rattled thunderously as a prelude to the emergence of a band of musicians in leopard-skins, playing a four-square march tune with a crude elemental pulse, who wheeled about at the foot of the ramp and divided into two groups, facing each other and marking time.

"Well, who would have thought it?" Guiseppe Ducci marvelled. He had been much impressed by the account his mother had given of Chart's work on Ilium. "Old Dr Lem—knowing somebody as famous as that!"

"He only knows somebody he knows," his father corrected absently, and went on staring through his binox, so that he did not notice the scowl his son bestowed on him.

It had taken Chevsky an eternity to make himself presentable: to shower, to dress neatly in the proper uniform, to organise the decorations on it, to fix his hangover, to cope with a depilator which kept trying to wander off across his scalp and carve deep ruts in his hair instead of confining itself to his cheeks and chin. He was as sweaty and ill-tempered at the end of the process as he had been at the beginning.

Stumbling up the rough track leading to the place

where the ship had landed, he heard the blaring of the fanfare, and cursed his wife to the uttermost hells of every planet he had ever heard of.

"We would not wish to delay your meeting with this friend of your friend," Speaker Kaydad said. That degree of acquaintance, in Yannish terms, was one of the closest; they tracked such contacts to the eighth degree as a matter of course.

Dr Lem forced a smile. It was hard. He was aware that everybody's eyes were on him—the eyes of a crowd as probably had not been seen on Yan since the arrival of the first Earthsider ship, if then—and he hated the sensation of being . . . What was the ancient phrase? Oh, yes: "in the beam".

Still, there was no alternative. He took his leave mechanically and set off towards the ship's ramp with Pompy, as ever, at his heels. The curve of the vessel loomed above him, its scale provoking the irrational fear that it might roll over him and crush him into a little wet smear. Behind its limb he saw a particularly brilliant meteorite stab down from the Ring towards Kralgak, visible against the daylight sky. He wished he hadn't noticed that. It was too much like an omen. This vast ship also had dropped out of heaven.

When he arrived within twenty metres of them, the honour guard and the band turned to face him, saluting a second time. He wondered optimistically whether Chart had picked on this approach because he believed Yan to be a backward planet. It was a slim hope. But any hope was better than none at all right now.

The instant he set foot on the ramp it began to carry him smoothly upwards, and Pompy also. Astonished, the chubble sat down, all her feet planted firmly on what should have been but was not solid ground, and let out a yowl of complaint. Bending absently to comfort her, he picked up one of the roses and examined it with a connoisseur's eyes. Amazing. "Peace", still breeding true after all these centuries.

Pompy licked it, and decided she didn't like that, either. She snuggled close against his leg for reassurance.

At the top of the ramp he found himself in a place not so much a lock, or even a hallway, as a grotto. From overhead draped stalactites hung, reminding him of the curtain effect which had opened last night's auroral display, lit from concealed sources to produce a bewildering range of light and shade. Water was running somewhere, and a lemony scent pervaded the air.

From among stone pillars flanking him, girls appeared in filmy robes, all beautiful, all graceful, who whispered welcome to him in a hundred soft individual voices. One in pale blue confronted him and urged him caressingly forward. He complied with a glance over his shoulder, and saw that the entrance to the ship had closed, as though it had never existed.

He looked again at the girl escorting him, meaning to put a question to her, and gave a gasp. He was no longer looking at a lovely blonde in a blue gown, but at a creature with green fangs and eyes like the glow of putrescent meat. A blast of brimstone assailed him, making his nostrils and throat sting; a braying noise like a mad donkey rang in his ears, and the hard floor under his feet turned to squelchy, nauseating mud.

Darkness fell.

But, paradoxically, Pompy continued to walk at his side, leaning slightly on his leg.

Hmm!

Dr Lem said after a pause, "There's no need to try and impress me, you know. And apparently you can't impress my chubble."

"Really?" a light voice countered from nowhere, in which sarcasm mingled with amusement. "Well, then, I'll stop the show. Although not many people benefit from an exclusive performance directed by Gregory

Chart, and I can assure you the opportunity will not recur."

Light sprang up, and there was no sign of the grotto or the girls. Dr Lem found himself in a huge plain open volume flanked by the supporting girders of the ship, facing and looking up towards a sort of translucent bubble from which the light emanated. On the front of the bubble, colossally magnified and distorted, was the face of a man with a beak-like nose, deep-set eyes, thick slightly shiny lips, skin like old parchment oiled and stretched on a frame of second-hand bone.

Pompy didn't like that either, and said so, very faintly.

"So you're Yigael Lem," said the ten-metre-high face. "Doyen of the human enclave here, so they tell me . . . Take the ascensor on your right, if you please."

The face began to shrink, drawing away. Head was joined by shoulders, then chest and arms, then a whole figure, still diminishing. Within the translucent globe, for one brief second, it looked as though some dreadfully overdue foetus were floating in luminous amniotic fluid.

Pompy absolutely refused to mount the ascensor, so he had to pick her up. Fortunately chubbles, although bulky, were light. Cradling her on his left arm, Dr Lem studied the globe in which Chart presented himself, and realised that it was the eye on the front of the ship's brain, pineally sunk inside the cranium of the hull. Its bulbous transparent surface was networked with the spider-tracery of non-refractive vidscreens; he counted automatically, found forty by thirty—twelve hundred possible different points of view which could be cast before Chart to make an insectile mosaic of the world.

Behind him was its retina: a panel four metres high on and through which he could dictate the course of his illusions, by speech, touch, throwing a shadow or any other means, as the whim took him. The rods and cones of sensors tactile, sonic, heat-responsive—for all Dr Lem knew, capable of detecting impulses directly from a human nervous system—jutted towards him, finer than fur.

The platform on which the ascensor debouched was overlooked by a railed gallery. Leaning on the rail, staring down at him, was a woman with a Salvadoran merlin on her wrist, a lovely savage creature of blood-red, green and grey. Impatient of its hood, it rustled its wings with a tinkle of the bells on its jesses.

The woman, strangely enough, was also hooded. But that was a fashion on certain planets, he had heard.

A chair appeared on the platform, fatly padded. Chart's voice, disembodied, invited him to sit down, and he complied, soothing Pompy, who had spotted the merlin and reacted badly. The curving wall of what he now thought of as the eye deformed Chart himself into a series of warped bows, as though his long bones had been softened and his whole body shaped anew under a roller, but it could be seen that he was thin, and that he was plainly dressed in a blue coat without ornament except a monogram in gold.

Dr Lem felt as though his mind were darting back and forth inside his skull, a mouse in a cage, finding no gap in the wire. Chart watched him lazily, making the translucent globe surrounding him seem like the objective of a microscope and his visitor a gratifying specimen.

Ask who our mutual friend is . . . ? Trivial. No, there's only one important question I must put.

Abruptly Dr Lem found his voice, and spoke up. "What brings you to Yan, Mr Chart?"

"This, chiefly," Chart said, and reached to his right with an arm that briefly elongated into a horrible curved line, then returned to near-normal bringing with it a cuboidal shape. Dr Lem recognised it at once, but was taken aback; it was so out of keeping with the advanced technical environment of this ship.

"A book?" he said uncertainly.

"Yes, a book! And one I feel sure you must know. Oh—I'm sorry; perhaps it's at an awkward angle for you to read the title and author's name." He turned the large oblong volume so that its spine was visible and well lit.

"Why, it's Marc Simon's version of the Mutine Epics!"

"Yes, indeed," Chart said with a smile. "Unusual to find even a poet's work being published in book form nowadays, isn't it? I'm told that it's due, in Simon's case, to the very limited demand for—but I digress. I was answering your question, wasn't I?"

At the distant edge of Dr Lem's awareness he fancied he could hear landslides. He said eventually, stroking Pompy with one hand all the time because the chubble was trembling, "You're not acquainted with the author?"

"Not yet. I intend to meet him. I presume he can be located, even though his publishers tell me he lives among the Yanfolk and not in the enclave. That must account for the insight of his translations, I suppose. To my inexpert eye they seem brilliant."

Dr Lem gave a distracted nod.

"Even though he has—ah—gone native, though, I doubt if he can be so withdrawn as to refuse to meet me. Or is he? Have I made my trip in vain?"

"Uh . . ." Dr Lem wanted to wipe his face; it was prickly with sweat, although the temperature here was mild and pleasant. He had assumed, directly he was shown the book, that Marc was the friend of a friend Chart had referred to, but if he had had a chance to reflect, he would have realised that was out of the question—he hadn't seen Marc among the crowd outside, but it was beyond doubt that Shyalee would have insisted on him coming here. So Chart could have called for him at once.

Who, then . . . ?

But the silence was dragging on unbearably. He said with an effort, "No, I imagine he'll be delighted that you like his work . . . However, you have scarcely come scores of parsecs for a social call."

"Admitted," Chart said with a chuckle.

"Then—"

"Oh, there's no need to beat about the bush with me, Dr Lem," Chart said with a sudden access of weariness. "I'm here because I'm alive and in good health, and I've been everywhere and done almost everything else. I'm looking for a new audience offering a new challenge."

The landslide in Dr. Lem's imagination turned to the crash of galaxies. He set his shoulders back, conscious of how ridiculous a figure he must cut: small and thin, against that vastly magnified form in the globe, with the furry chubble draped across his chest like a stole.

He said, "You must not come looking for it here."

"And why not?"

"Because . . . Well, because I have been on Hyrax. And how long ago were *you* there? Sixty years?"

"Ah, Hyrax!" Chart echoed softly. "Yes, some have said that was my masterpiece. But I can't live in the shade of past achievements, you know. For me, the next one is always going to be my best."

"The next one will have to be somewhere other than on Yan," Dr. Lem insisted. "With the example of what you've done to disrupt human worlds before us, we dare not risk—"

Abruptly Chart's expression was very stern; his eyes narrowed, his lips pressed into a thin line.

"Since when has this planet been your property? I didn't come here to talk with Dr Lem, or any other human. I came here to perform for the Yanfolk, and what I do will be entirely up to them."

Dr Lem sat very still. Because he knew what the decision of the Yanfolk was going to be—Speaker Kaydad had come to tell him, to ask for his support.

Against all the odds, against the logic which had brought him to the contrary conclusion at once, not just the Earth-worshipping youngsters but also the grave, conservative elders did want Gregory Chart to perform on Yan.

Perhaps that noise in his mind wasn't the clash of galaxies after all. Perhaps it was smaller, but closer: the shattering of a moon.

VIII

At long last Dr Lem said, "So the temptation to play at being a god has finally got the better of you, has it?"

For an instant he thought he had contrived to make Chart lose his temper; he leaned forward within his globe, and his head and shoulders deformed towards the hugeness Dr Lem had first seen, the monstrous embryonic forehead looming over the small full-lipped mouth.

He recovered quickly. But there had been that brief breach in his composure, and Dr Lem resolved to exploit it if he could.

"To play at being a god, did you say? Dr Lem, I expected more insight from a man like you. You are a psychologist, are you not? Then you should be able to recognise my particular breed of ambition. It's not in the least megalomaniac. It's—well, the drive towards maximum realisation of my capacities. I told you: I've done almost everything I've ever wanted to. There's very little left that offers me a fresh challenge."

"Your existing audiences have grown bored with you, then? Or have your imitators overtaken you and squeezed you out?" Dr Lem made the words deliberately sarcastic, hoping to wound Chart's *amour propre*.

But they glanced off him harmlessly, for he laughed.

"It must be the fact that you've spent too long among the Yanfolk. I'm told they're fantastically courteous and peaceable. You've forgotten how to frame an insult, haven't you? Not that there are many insults which can touch me . . . Still, I'll dispose of your objections anyhow. It may simplify matters.

"No, I have not been 'squeezed out' by any imitators. I have some. They are all inferior. My audiences are not bored with me; every world where humans have settled has hired me at least once, and every single one is begging me to come back—yes, before you interrupt, that does include Hyrax!"

"I find that hard to believe," said Dr Lem.

"Do you? Yes, I can see why." Chart rubbed his chin with a horribly distorted hand. "I presume you were there after my visit?"

"Yes."

"Had you also been there before?"

Dr Lem swallowed and shook his head.

"I doubted that you had. Under the Quains there was little chance to visit the planet." Chart made an expansive gesture. "I'll tell you how I saw it when I first arrived: a devilish tyranny, excused on the grounds that it offered 'security' and 'peace'. Every man, woman and child on Hyrax was hung about with invisible fetters, branded the private property of Elias Quain as surely as if a hot iron had been seared into their cheeks. True or false?"

"So you're presenting yourself as a disinterested liberator?" gibed Dr Lem. But his heart was not in the words, and his tone betrayed him.

"I am not. The people of Hyrax paid me, every penny of the sum agreed by the Quains. They felt it was well worth bleeding themselves in their own interests for a change, after so many centuries of being bled by their rulers. They were paying in arrears, and they admitted it, for their own stupidity and sloth."

"If you feel proud of rescuing people from that sort of predicament, are there no other chances for you to do so?" Dr Lem countered. "I could name half a dozen worlds where the situation—"

"So could I, so could I, so could I!" Chart cut in. "But I've just told you: that is not what I am. I did it once, almost incidentally. Why should I do it again, even if I am proud that I was instrumental in freeing Hyrax? I don't repeat myself—I leave repetition to my silly imitators. I, Gregory Chart, *create!*"

The head drew back inside the globe, and two clenched fists rose before the magnified face, pounding knuckles against knuckles.

Looking at him, Dr Lem thought: *This is the most dangerous man in the galaxy. Artists have always been dangerous. But with this much talent and this much power . . .*

He said suddenly, "But you won't find what you want here. This is an ancient world. There's no chance to create on Yan—only to . . ."

"Imitate?" Chart supplied softly.

"I was hesitating to use the word. But—yes."

There was a pause. Eventually Chart said, not looking towards Lem but into vacant space, "Yes, in one sense that may be true. Nonetheless, don't you see that that would furnish *me* with a new challenge? I've performed for every human-occupied world. What's left to me? I'm not worn out, I'm not old! Oh, in years, I suppose I am, but not up here inside my head! My brain heaves and surges like a wild beast in a cage, conceiving and aborting a score of ideas every day! I can carve a sun's corona into strange and lovely shapes, create poems in plasma, and—yes, I have passed time in doing that. But for whom? Who can watch me? Who can appreciate what I do on that scale? Am I to perform for myself and the dumb churning audience of the stars? Shall I tackle colossal simple tasks, tug the stars into new constellations? I think I could; the last contract I had was with Tubalcain, the payment is still not exhausted, and if I chose I could take the balance in the machines I'd need. What for? To leave myself a monument, a constellation in the sky of some abandoned planet which will spell my name to the first explorers when they get there? I don't want a monument! I'm an artist, Dr Lem! I need an audience, the most discerning, the most discriminating, the most responsive I can find! I've used up all of them . . . bar one."

"An audience of another species," said Dr Lem. The sound of his own words made him shiver.

"Yes." Chart licked his lips. "Yes, I have never satisfied an alien audience. And I think—I have to believe—that I can."

"Papa!" Guiseppe said. "Give me the binox for a moment. The go-board is active again."

Ducci swung around, raising the binox to his own eyes instead, and a moment later roared, "Quick! Go and— No, *diavolo!* Too late, too late!"

He rounded on his son furiously. "You said you'd tied it up for hours—that news-machine!"

Flinching back from his father's sudden unaccountable rage, Giuseppe said, "But I did! I sent it on a wild-goose chase!"

"Then why is it over there at the board, in terminal emergency mode?"

"What?" Giuseppe seized the binox and stared through them. True enough. On the edge of the go-board, the obsolescent machine was taking itself systematically to bits: individual sections each primed with the same condensed news-item and a different route across the board.

"Now the whole galaxy will know Chart has come

here!" Ducci fumed. "We'll be inundated! Oh, you—you . . . !"

"Oh, shut up, papa!" his son snapped. "Chart had probably told everyone already. A man like him must have news-machines at his heels wherever he goes. Maybe that one came here because of him."

"I guess so," Ducci admitted reluctantly after a few moments' reflection. "But all the same it makes me *mad!* Why couldn't the bastard have gone somewhere else?"

"Why are you so angry about him coming to Yan?" Giuseppe countered. "Surely it's—"

There was a shout, and they glanced around to find Warden Chevsky approaching them, obviously out for someone's blood.

Behind the deforming globe, Chart shifted on his chair and brought his face and limbs into newly weird arrangements. He said, "Before we go any further, let me dispose of all the other objections I suspect you're going to advance. The question of payment will not arise—as I told you, I have a vast amount of credit on Tubalcain, enough, if I spin it out, to last me the rest of my life."

Dr Lem nodded. He had never been to Tubalcain, but it was notoriously the galaxy's most industrialised planet: almost intolerable to live on because everything right down to water and oxygen had to be manufactured, but so dedicated to technology that its output of desirable goods supported half a dozen other planets' needs. Its products were even exported to Earth.

He made a mental note to check the encyclopedia and find out what the people there had hired Chart to do.

"Also," Chart pursued, "I imagine you've considered getting up a petition, or something, to have me legally removed from Yan. You can't. Earthsiders here are on sufferance. Legally and actually the authority resides with the natives. I'm prepared to take my chances with them. And you can't keep me from meeting and talking to them, can you?"

"No, of course not. You and your staff have the same rights as if you'd come off the go-board in conventional fashion—"

"Staff?" Chart cut in. He curled his lip. "I have no *staff!* I did have, long ago, but one by one they decided they could do better on their own after milking my brains, and they drifted away. And one by one they found out that they couldn't. Some have begged to be taken back, and I've always refused them. I've learned to do without them—without anyone, indeed, except my mistress."

He gestured, and Lem turned automatically to look at the woman on the gallery. She raised the hand which did not carry the merlin as though to unhood it. Instead, after a second of hesitation, she removed her own hood.

"Remember me, Yigael?" she said.

Time stopped.

Since nobody had disturbed him—one couldn't count the interruption caused by the news-machine—and the streets outside were still quiet, Erik Svitra decided to look over the house he'd wandered into and see how these people lived. He had inspected four or five of the house's nine rooms before he suddenly realised that it wasn't the squalid little hovel he had assumed; it was meant for *one* family.

He didn't believe it at first. Back where he came from, a place this size would never have been built, but the larger structures that were built averaged three or four rooms per family.

So *that* was why they had single-form furniture! No point in having items that changed their shape and texture, if you had enough space to store separate units for each domestic purpose. Old-fashioned, maybe, but at least it meant you didn't have to squabble over whether you should or shouldn't change the eatoff into a lieon now, or later.

And that thing over there, that he'd taken for a funny arrangement of shelves: that must be a staircase! No ascensor to reach the upper story—but, on the other hand, no exercisers in the children's playroom, either. They must get their exercise on the stairs, lifting their own weight against this Earth-force gravity, and maybe even running and jumping, right out in the open.

Hmm!

He rubbed his chin thoughtfully. He'd been wondering why anyone should choose to come to this one enclosed corner of a world full of funny aliens, instead of a human-controlled planet. All of a sudden he was wondering the exact opposite: why the place wasn't cram-jammed with people in search of the quiet life and the good old-type luxuries. Of course, there were probably drawbacks: insects, maybe, or cold weather, or—what was the term?—rain.

Still, there was one thing in the place that was bang up to date: a communet terminal with as wide a range of facilities as he'd seen anywhere. He ran his finger over the board, counting news, encyclopedia, personcall, conference, real-time entertainment, home-help, and library options. Almost absent-mindedly, he chose encyclopedia, and then tapped out the name CHART, GREGORY.

Just to see if the facilities were as good as they looked.

When Dr Lem descended the ship's ramp again, he found that the roses had gone, and the soldiers, and the musicians. There was nothing but the plain grey ramp. Delighted to be back in the open air, Pompy wriggled out of his arms and raced ahead down it to the ground, not even minding when she was pitched off the end because she misjudged the speed of travel and rolled over in the dust. She might almost have been a kit again.

Calling her to heel, he set off the way he had come, and realised with a start that there was no one waiting at the foot of the ramp to demand what he and Chart had talked about. Instead, there was a dense crowd of people with their backs to him, about a hundred metres off. Some sort of trouble, he read from their nervous gestures.

Abruptly Hector Ducci caught sight of him and strode to meet him. Others followed: his son Giuseppe, and those of the people of the enclave that Dr Lem would have termed *responsible*—in other words, those who would at once have realised the danger of Chart coming here, without being even briefly blinded by the man's reputation. He saw Toshi Shigaraku—her husband Jack was still lecturing his pupils—and Pedro Phillips too. All except Harriet Pokorod, the medical doctor.

Giuseppe outstripped the others on his young legs, and called, "Dr Lem! A terrible thing has happened!"

"There are going to be plenty of terrible things happening," Dr Lem said. "So how has the sequence begun?"

"It's Warden Chevsky! He's beaten up his wife! Right out in the open where everyone could see—caught her by the hair and just *hit* her!"

"That's right!" his father confirmed, catching up. "Never saw anything so disgusting—like something out of the Dark Ages! Seems he was drunk last night, and slept clear through the show in the sky, everything. Blames her for not waking him up!"

"Harriet's tending Sidonie now," Pedro Phillips supplemented. "But he cut her lip open, blacked her eye . . . Ach!"

"And we'd better get you away from here," Ducci muttered. "He's furious because you were invited on board. Thinks he ought to have been the first to greet Chart— Say! What did you talk about?"

"It's not so much what we talked about," Dr Lem answered. "It's more who he has with him."

"Staff?" Ducci frowned. "You mean a lot of them—?"

"No, there's just his mistress and himself. The brain of that ship is so far in advance of anything else I've seen I can scarcely believe it. He said his last contract was with Tubalcain, so I guess he took it in part-payment." Dr Lem rubbed his eyes. The sun, despite its halo, was very bright out here.

"But it's his mistress's name. Hector, you may not remember her, but I'm sure Pedro does. Morag Feng?"

"She came back?" Phillips said in disbelief, and his jaw hinged open and hung foolish-wide.

IX

RED-EYED FROM LACK of sleep, his belly rumbling with indefinable apprehension, Marc Simon wandered across the rough ground beyond the spaceport, clutching the dictyper which he invariably carried so that he could note down things he saw or promising turns of phrase which occurred to him. Shyalee had insisted that they come out of town, along with everybody else, to look at the giant ship resting on its bed of yellowish crushed rock like the egg of some impossible dinosaur, so he had complied, and they had duly stood around with everybody else watching it do nothing, until she grew bored and tried to persuade him to join the cluster of apes surrounding Rayvor-Harry and Alice Ming. The latter was holding forth with authority about Chart's work, though Marc was sure she had never actually seen any.

So he had left Shyalee to her own devices and set off at random in the direction of the Mutine Mandala. After he had gone some distance, he had heard a blast of music from behind him, and glanced back to see that there was at long last something happening around the ship . . . but he had decided to keep going.

He had also noticed that the go-board was active; that, though, was nothing extraordinary. It was, after all, spring again, and every spring a handful of people wandered across the board to Yan to escape winter on their own planet, or perhaps a winter state of mind which lasted the year around.

That chubby stranger he and Shyalee had encountered rising from the shelter of a bush, for example, with some kind of salve newly dried on his bare brown legs. Marc frowned. He had been so preoccupied he had scarcely noticed the fellow. Freelance drug-tester, hadn't he said? In that case, if he was here after a sample of *sheyashrim,* someone ought to warn him off . . . or perhaps not. Perhaps he should be left to find out for himself. Marc didn't much care for the scouts who toured the worlds looking for new ways of hiding reality from people. On the other hand, one must be tolerant; it was a big galaxy, as the saying went, with room for all types.

And he was not the one to criticise, not after what he had nearly done last night at Goydel's.

The path he followed took him along the meeting-line of Blaw and Rhee; one side of him were inhospitable rocks, the other gardens and orchards, both stretching for hundreds of kilometres. Trees here and there stood proud to the sun, and there were numerous brooks, miniature tributaries of the Smor. He came to one and followed it absently, a narrow pebbly stream fringed with plants like blue moss and populated by organisms neither plant nor animal, which spent most of the year as sessile flowers but with the advent of spring drew up their roots and set off, snail-slow, in search of more favourable locations.

In a while he chanced on a smooth rock overlooking the stream and sat down on it, his back firmly to the direction he had come from. For a long time—he had no idea how long—he stared at the sun-glint on the water so fixedly that when he blinked he saw it again with colours reversed inside his lids.

Abruptly he started the dictyper and spoke to it. An uncritical machine was the only audience with which he could share his present doubts.

"How is it that I feel this visit of Chart's to be both inevitable and disastrous?

"Well, I guess it was inevitable that he would ultimately feel the attraction of performing for an alien species. I've never seen him at work, but I've seen the impact his performance on Hyrax had left half a century later, so I have a clear idea of the scale he operates on. I don't know if he's what some people call him—the greatest artist of all time—but there's no disputing one of his achievements. He's carved out a whole new medium of expression, and instead of what usually happens, someone coming up from behind almost at once and improving on the pioneer's experiments, he's kept ahead of everyone else including the competitors who studied under him.

"Which seems to make people working in other fields feel insecure. I know I've been hearing patronising remarks about him all my life. I guess it must be the same kind of thing as you'd have found when the first person cast a statue in bronze and other sculptors realised what was wrong with stone, or when fixed images on tape and—oh, what's the word? Not layer, not skin . . . Got it! Film! I mean when stage-directors found tape and film competing with the disposition of live actors on a set.

"So here he is, a galaxy-wide public figure, who only needs to set course for an inhabited system and the news runs ahead of him and—and provokes debates in the planetary congress! So the temptation to perform for a non-human audience must be a terrific challenge for him.

"But that's not why I think of his arrival on Yan as being *inevitable*. More . . ."

Marc hesitated, wondering whether what he was about to record would sound silly, then ploughed on doggedly.

"More, his very existence is a Yannish kind of idea. He is, I guess, a dramatist. But he's so much more than just that. He's about as near as we humans have ever come to realising the implications of that term which they introduced, long before I reached here, to translate the epithet given to the—the heroes, the protagonists, the whatever-the-hell, who dominate the Mutine Epics. Like them, Gregory Chart is a dramaturge."

And what does that mean? Having the word is very useful; it's pregnant with associations and I'm obliged to whoever coined it. But—!

He sighed and shut off the machine. Coming back to the real world, after an absence much longer than he had intended, he glanced about him and discovered how short the shadows were.

Why, it must be almost mid-day. And here he was practically on the threshold of the Mutine Mandala!

Thought and action coincided, almost in panic. It had been months, more than a year perhaps, since he had seen the Mutine Flash from this close. And he had meant to experience it a second time from inside the mandala, having worked his way back to it by slow daily degrees, and somehow . . .

He thrust that memory aside, and all the recollected sins of omission which trailed behind it, and considered the hill he had been breasting as he followed the course of the brook upstream. Near its crest stood a substantial ghul-tree, whose nuts formed a staple of the Yannish diet. Its branches were broad and evenly spaced, a natural ladder. He headed for it promptly. Up there, fifteen or twenty metres above the ground, he ought to be able to see clear across the Blaw Plateau to the point where the back of the land broke and began its five-hundred-kilometre slide, imperceptibly gradual, to the shore of the Gheb Salt Lake. There were other towns and cities in that direction, some of them larger than Prell, but none having so handsome a location on so broad a river.

He stretched up to take hold of the first foliage-shaded branch, and something stabbed at his fingers.

He cried out and leapt away, a trickle of blood running over his knuckles. Staring up into the twilight among the branches, he made out something moving, heard rustling sounds.

A bird? But this is Yan! There are no birds!

Then, from behind him, a voice called, "Oh, I'm sorry! Did he hurt you?"

Hurrying up the rise with a swish of boots came a woman in skin-tight green, nearly as tall as himself, hair the shade of beaten copper drawn back from her long face with a clip of jet. On one wrist she wore a leather cuff decorated with diamonds.

Marc stared at her stupidly, not wondering why he hadn't seen her before—if one person had wandered across the go-board to Yan today, so might another have—but why he hadn't seen her *before*. Being that tall, she would have had to lie down and grovel in order to . . .

Oh. On her hip: the golden glint of an anti-see unit—expensive, and on many planets illegal. But not uncommon.

She asked again, with a hint of impatience, "*Are* you hurt?"

"I . . . " He looked at his hand, shook the blood away to expose the injury, and found a mere scratch. "Uh—no, I guess not badly."

"If it was his beak, not to worry. It's his talons that may cause infection. Though every time he perches on my wrist they're automatically cleaned, of course. Home, you evil creature, home, home! So-o-o! Home, home, home!"

She reached up into the dimness of the tree. With a

muttered complaint the bird flapped towards her wrist, and she dexterously hooded him.

"There!" she said, turning back to Marc. "He won't apologise on his own behalf, so I'd better. He always resents the first flighting on a new planet, and thinks it and everything about it is out to persecute him. Very paranoid creatures, these!"

"But beautiful," Marc said, having stripped a leaf from the tree to wrap around his cut finger. Ghul-leaves were useful to assist clotting, if you were among the lucky five per cent of humans who were not allergic to them. "What is he?"

"Oh, a Salvadoran merlin. Away back when, some-one had the bright idea that hawking would be valuable on underdeveloped planets without roads or tracks, not only for hunting but for herding and guarding stock. So he started tinkering with the genetics of all the hawks he could get hold of. One line escaped and bred in the wild, and this one's ancestors were among them. Owing to which he's inherited an exaggerated sense of his own importance—haven't you, you vicious brute?" She jogged her wrist, and the merlin clacked his beak.

Marc had continued to stare, more at her than the bird, while she was speaking. There was something vaguely familiar about her, as though he had seen a pic-ture of her long ago, but he couldn't place it. He had had time to form an impression of her as a person now, and for some reason he could not express clearly to himself he found he didn't care for the reaction she pro-voked in him. Her voice was brittle, the words coming over-quickly, and there had been impatience in her tone when she asked the second time if he was hurt . . . He chided himself. He was over-reacting. He had spent so long here on Yan, first in the already leisurely envi-ronment of the enclave, then among the Yanfolk whose life had a stately, predetermined quality, that he was probably out of the habit of dealing with people from tenser backgrounds.

He was on the point of asking where she was from, and whether she had come across the board simply to find a place where she could fly her merlin, when he realized that she was in her turn staring at him.

"I—am—a—cretin," she said deliberately. He started.

"Two kinds of cretin. Three!" She took a pace closer to him. "Damnation, you're wearing a *heyk* and *welwa*, and it's taken me this long to register the fact!"

"I . . . " Marc put his hand up to the breast of the Yannish cape.

"And unless a tattoo-artist or a skin-grafter has moved in here and given those apes what they most want, got rid of their dark patches—in which case you would *not* be wearing that outfit—you're an Earthsider."

Her eyes were very dark green, Marc saw, with the same piercing quality as those of her merlin.

"In which case there's only one person you can be. You're Marc Simon."

It took a very long time to play the article on Chart. Partway through, Erik was so fascinated, he forgot about the risk of someone coming in and disturbing him; he pulled up a chair and sat down before the screen, almost gaping. No wonder they'd gone to look at the starship!

He had never been much interested in the creative arts. His tastes lay more in the direction of the subjective ones—those which came in a pill, a powder, a gas or an injector. But it looked as though when this character Chart set to work, the mind got blown to shreds right out on the objective level!

And, he thought as the article concluded with a reference to a contract on Tubalcain which specified that if you wanted to view a tape of the performance there you had to pay a separate fee, *that word "blown" re-*

minded me of a point I wanted to check on. How does one get a Yannish girl and is it worth it?

After some cogitation, he tapped out the article "Yan," sub-category "Inter-species relations", sub-sub-category "Sex". The informat was capable of selecting the proper title if he'd guessed wrong. But all he got was a blank screen, and it dawned on him that, living right here on Yan as they did, the people of the human enclave probably didn't need to find that sort of information through the communet.

"I—uh . . ." Marc's voice sounded creaky in his own ears. "How did you know?"

"I'm Morag Feng—mistress of Gregory Chart." That name rang a faint chord in memory, like the face, but he still could not identify it. "I've read your translation of the Mutine Epics. I was the one who gave it to Gregory, and that's what brought him here, your book!"

Marc felt dazed. He said, "Chart—uh—Chart liked my work?"

"Liked it!" With a harsh laugh. "It's the only real translation anyone's ever done of a non-human poem! Here, come on back to the ship with me, right away! I'll call Gregory and tell him I've run into you. He'll be delighted. You're the person he most wants to talk to on this planet . . . Is something wrong?"

She checked in the act of lifting a communet extension to her mouth, a miniature one which hung at her waist on the side opposite her anti-see unit.

"I'm—I'm just overwhelmed," Marc said faintly. "Especially since that translation is terrible. I rushed into it when I'd hardly had time to settle down here. Thought I knew everything about Yan and the Yannish language. It wasn't until I moved out of the enclave that I realised how crude, how clumsy, how superficial it all was!" He clenched his fists in frustration.

"Well, it brought Gregory here," Morag said tartly.

"And that's something to your credit, isn't it? Come on!"

"Actually, I . . ." Marc glanced over his shoulder. The sun was very close to the zenith now. "I was hoping to wait and see the Mutine Flash at noon. That's—"

"Yes, I know about the Flash," she interrupted. "But you'll have lots more chances to see it. And if all goes well, before long you'll understand what it is, what it's for."

"What?" That took Marc's breath away completely.

"You heard me!" She seized his arm and began to hurry him along beside her, towards the ship. "What do you think Gregory came here to *do*?"

X

"MORAG FENG?" SAID Giuseppe in a baffled tone. "I guess I heard the name somewhere, but—"

"Hey! Lem's out! Let me get at him!"

A roar in the unmistakable voice of Chevsky. The little group swung to face the direction it had come from, and they saw the warden forcing his way between the close-packed ranks of those who had reverted to an ancient habit-pattern and gathered around Sidonie while Harriet Pokorod was ministering to her wounds.

Chevsky's expression was halfway between sheepishness and arrogance, and he was doing his best to make the latter come out on top. Directly on his heels six or eight other people followed. As the community's psychologist, Dr Lem was strict in not permitting himself likes and dislikes; if he had been able to indulge such luxuries, though, these were the ones he would have detested. Just as Chevsky craved the trappings of authority so much that he had come to what he regarded as a backwater purely because he could hold down a job with a title that he would never have been considered for elsewhere, so these compensated for the smallness of their puddle by trying to be big frogs. In particular, he noticed Dellian Smith and his wife, who were so ashamed of their jobs as sewage and purification experts—no matter how indispensable, how valuable, their specialty—that they had become intimate cronies of Chevsky and would barely associate with the rest of the enclave.

Oh, why do human beings have to be so touchy and pompous?

With heavy menacing strides Chevsky closed the gap and confronted Dr Lem. Pompy, sensing that he intended her master harm, rose up on all her many feet, hoisted her fur into the extreme defensive mode which made it as stiff and prickly as a porcupine's quills, and opened her mouth to display her fangs. But she was old, and the fangs were blunt and unimpressive.

"Warden!" A cry from behind Chevsky, and here, following him and his companions, came Harriet Pokorod, trying to re-pack her medical bag as she hastened along.

Chevsky ignored her. He planted his hands on his hips and rasped, "Well, at least you're not trying to dodge me—not that you could! I know you like to take our heads apart behind the scenes, work out our weak points, tinker with us until we can't call our brains our own, but this time you've gone too far!"

There was a dead pause. Then: "What in the galaxy are you talking about?" demanded Hector Ducci.

Chevsky favoured him with a withering glare. "You know damned well what I mean—Sidonie and your wife are thick as thieves! You know Sid's been going behind my back to talk to this shrivelled bag of bones, gabbing about things that ought to be personal between husband and wife! So don't try and convince *me* it wasn't due to him that she left me asleep when everyone else knew Chart had arrived! Don't tell me it was an accident that the warden was the last to know we had such a distinguished visitor, and this scarecrow Lem was the first to be invited aboard his ship!"

"And don't try getting back at the warden here for what he did to Sidonie, either!" Dellian Smith interjected. "If I'd been in his shoes I'd have done the same."

"Quite right too!" his wife said with asperity.

A period of hostile silence. During it, quite distinctly, Dr Lem heard Toshi's teeth chattering.

At length he said, having honed the words, "Well, it wouldn't have made too good an impression if the first person Chart met here was staggering drunk."

The time for delicacy was over. There had to be axes as well as scalpels.

Chevsky turned purple. Before he could speak, though, Dr Lem hurried on. "No one who wasn't intoxicated could have slept through what happened last night! Pedro?"

"Right," the merchant said, taking his stand at Dr Lem's side. "He bought six litres of assorted liquors from me last time he called by."

"And he's my biggest client for the kind of minor analgesics and stomach-pills you need to take care of the morning after," Harriet said, having finally replaced everything in her medical kit and come around to take the corresponding place on Dr Lem's other side. In her haste, she almost trod on Pompy, and had to apologise and pet her—an impulse she regretted, because the chubble was still in defensive mode and her fur was sharp.

"Doesn't a man with a wife like Sid have the right to drown his sorrows now and then?" Dellian Smith countered. But his heart wasn't in it; the words rang false. In any case Chevsky had decided not to let himself be baited.

"Shut up!" he said, jabbing Smith in the ribs. "I didn't come here to talk about that. Even if Sid does gossip about it to this bastard Lem, I think my private life is my affair! I'm not proud of the way that woman acts, but it's up to me to take care of it as I see fit.

Marital discord isn't grounds to impeach me, you know that, and if I drink now and then, so what? Doesn't interfere with my duties!"

He glared at the trio facing him: the psychologist, the merchant and the medical doctor. At their backs Ducci was hovering, uncertain whether he should declare his sympathies or whether, as technical supervisor of the enclave, he was better advised to remain neutral. Dr Lem hoped fervently he would choose the latter course.

"No, what's really important right now," Chevsky continued, "is something else. It's this impression everyone has that there's a self-appointed caucus which wants to prevent Chart from performing here."

Vigorous nods from the Smiths and those beside them. It wasn't hard to deduce who "everyone" must be.

Chevsky set his shoulders back and jutted his jaw aggressively. "Now I admit right away I never saw Chart working! But I have been talking with a lot of people who did—your wife among them, Ducci!" With a scowl. "I don't have to be a genius to realise his work is epoch-making. Having Chart perform on your planet is—well, it's kind of a landmark. A historical event! And I can judge the feeling in the enclave when it comes to something big, something important. So I'm here to tell you straight out: if you try and obstruct Chart, prevent him from performing here, you're going to find every last mother's son on the other side from you—you self-important prigs!"

The Smiths nodded again, and so did his other companions. They put on expressions which apparently were attempts to duplicate Chevsky's, and waited for a response.

"But he doesn't have the least intention of performing for us," Dr Lem said after the lapse of a few seconds.

"What?" Chevsky took half a pace forward.

"What makes you think he'd regard three hundred people as worth his trouble? Would you expect him to, when he performs for continents, for whole planets?"

"You mean—" Chevsky began, but Smith shouldered past him.

"You mean the bastard wants to mount a show for the apes?" His tone was wringing wet with disgust and horror.

As though intended to answer precisely that question, once again Chart's voice rang out from the ship.

"It has been perceived that three most distinguished members of the Yannish community of Prell are present, Speaker Kaydad, *Hrath* Vetcho and *Hrath* Goydel!"

"Does he even speak Yannish?" Harriet muttered under her breath.

"You'd expect him to bone up on everything about this planet before coming here, wouldn't you?" Phillips answered equally softly.

"Should it be the desire of these gentlemen to enter the ship, it will delight Gregory Chart to entertain them on board!"

"Hey!" Ducci started. "What about showing advanced technology to non-humans . . . ?" His voice trailed away. He knew, as well as anyone else in earshot, that raising a trivial charge like that against Chart was a waste of time. This man had been writing his own laws for well over half a century.

He lifted his binox and peered through them. After a moment he said, "Yes, there they go."

Chevsky, the Smiths and their companions, exchanged looks of amazement and dismay.

"Well, we'll see about *that!*" the warden exclaimed at length, and stormed away.

"But it isn't really Chart we have to worry about," Dr Lem said at last.

"What?" Harriet glanced from one to another of their uniformly depressed faces.

"Morag Feng's on board," Phillips said. "She's Chart's mistress now."

"Oh, *no!*" Harriet's square, sensible face paled, and she let her medical kit fall to the full stretch of her arm.

"What the hell is all this about Morag Feng?" Ducci demanded. "I have this vague idea I heard the name, but . . ."

"It would have been just before your time," Dr Lem said wearily, passing his hand through his shock of hair. "I'd been here for—let me see—yes, about fourteen years, so that would make it eighteen years ago. But you knew her, Pedro, didn't you?"

The merchant gave an emphatic nod. "She wandered across the board to Yan the summer after I brought the family here. I remember her very well."

"And about two months before Alice came," Harriet supplied in a tight voice.

"My—*no!*" Ducci clenched his fists. "She's never the woman Alice stole Rayvor from?"

"She is indeed," Dr Lem said sadly. "And she hasn't grown out of her hatred, either. I'm sure of that."

Fool! Idiot! Cretin! Self-directed insults marked time with Erik's footsteps as he plodded back the way he had come into the town, stooped under the weight of his pack. Of course he ought to have recognised the name Chart—instantly! He ought to have taken personal credit for identifying him to the news-machine, and then he could have lodged a fee-claim at the local informat, and, assuming Chart was really as newsworthy as the encyclopedia had indicated, he'd have had credit in store to get him off Yan if he drew a blank as far as drugs were concerned.

Imbecile!

He stopped dead in his tracks. While he was using the communet in that house where he'd taken the food, why had he not dialled the article on the drug he was investigating? It would have saved him an immense amount of trouble. There was a limit to the amount of off-planet information one could store in an encyclopedia; there were strict conditions regulating the priority accorded to types of data, as a result, so back where Erik had come from on Ilium, there had been one reference to the *sheyashrim* drug, and that merely in passing, during a description of one of these sadistic orgies, or whatever, in which so many of the Yanfolk apparently got killed. There were plenty of planets where sadistic orgies were in vogue, and most of them were more than averagely wealthy. Hence his visit.

And obviously, right here on Yan, there ought to be a higher priority assigned to local information than—

He was on the point of turning around and heading straight back for the nearest empty human house, to consult the communet again. Up ahead, though, he suddenly realised there were loud voices—human—raised in excited conversation. He blinked. Five or six people were approaching, and at their head, the same warden he'd woken up without planning to.

"Hey!" the warden shouted, spotting him. "Hey, look there! That's the guy who did me the good turn, woke me and told me Chart was here when Sid had sneaked off and left me! Say, feller!"

Beaming, he advanced with an air of forced joviality. Erik sighed, let his pack slide to the ground, and offered his hand.

"Morag Feng," Ducci said, twisting his mouth around the name as though it were bitter. "I did hear about her . . . but it was a long time ago." And he added to Giuseppe, "You were just a baby, then!"

"But I heard the name too," his son countered. "I get this idea she caused a considerable ruction, right?"

"I remember all the details," Dr Lem said quietly. "In a way, possibly some of what happened was my fault. Shall I tell you what I recall?"

"Please!" Ducci said. The others agreed, and Harriet appended a comment of her own.

"It's not the sort of data you can consult the commu-net for, is it?"

"I guess not," Dr Lem admitted, giving a skeletal smile at the black humour of the remark. "Well . . . Well, basically it happened this way. The enclave was relatively new, then—I myself came in with the second wave after it was set up, as you know, and it was still making occasional news: the first-ever human settlement on a planet dominated by another species. And, of course, our sexual compatibility was bringing in all kinds of disturbed persons, who caused terrible trouble. Didn't they, Harriet?"

The medical doctor snorted loudly.

"This Morag Feng was not a kink, really, but not very stable, either. She had theories about the dramaturges, the ancient Yannish civilisation, and the rest of it, and she was determined to prove herself right. She arrived, she declined to live among the people of the enclave, and she took a Yannish lover. Rayvor. In fact it was from her he learned the name Harry which he uses now.

"And then Alice Ming turned up—who did want to live in the enclave, who also wanted a Yannish lover, but preferred him to be . . ." Dr Lem hesitated. "Subservient? I think that's about right.

"Morag—I know this, because I was her confidant, and I guess I was more than a little in love with her myself . . . Morag wanted to find out, right away, what if anything the truth was behind the Mutine Epics, the wats and mandalas and so forth. So she went off and lay on the floor of the Mutine Mandala during the Flash."

A moment's silence. Ducci said at length, "The way Marc Simon did, the other year?"

"Yes. And you know what it did to him—drove him crazy for about three weeks, didn't it? He said it was like compressing a lifetime of psychedelic experience into thirty seconds."

"And he got terrible sunburn," Harriet muttered.

"But Morag's tall, muscular," Dr Lem said. "Alice is thin and delicate. More to Yannish taste. Alice saw her chance, and took Rayvor away while Morag was wandering around the Plateau of Blaw, gibbering to herself and screaming if anybody came near. When she recovered, she came and stayed with me for a while, needing a shoulder to weep on, and I persuaded her to go back across the board to some other world. And she did. And now she's back. And she's brought Gregory Chart with her. I repeat that, I emphasise that: *that is the woman who has brought Gregory Chart to Yan!*"

XI

"GREGORY'S ENGAGED WITH a delegation of Yanfolk,"
Morag whispered as she and Marc drew closer to the
ship. "I'll take you aboard anyway."

She had turned her anti-see unit back on and put her
arm around his waist to ensure that its field would en-
velop them both.

With half of his mind, Marc wanted to run like hell.
With the other, and dominant, half, he wanted to meet
Chart. He wanted—*needed*—to hear someone famous
for his artistic brilliance compliment him on the work
he had done on Yan. The natives didn't go in for ful-
some compliments; at most, they sighed, or smiled, or
arranged that the next time an especially successful
poet—artist—musician—talker appeared at a soirée,
the audience was slightly larger.

It was slim rations for a human being.

But on the way back to where the ship rested, he had
begun to hear the faint bells of memory rung by his
companion's name echo louder and louder, and—just
about at the point where the ship was clearly visible—
he had identified the mental reference. Harriet Pokorod
was talking as she dressed the sunburn, untended for al-

most three weeks, on his arms and legs and face. And she was saying that the last time she had a similar case . . .

Yes, he had recalled correctly. Morag Feng was the name of the woman who had come to Yan more than ten years before his own arrival, perhaps twelve years earlier, and lived among the Yanfolk and tried to experience the impact of the Mutine Flash.

His own head reeled when he merely thought of the single time he himself had undergone that terrifying ordeal. When the sun was at a certain angle relative to the mandala's crystal shafts, something happened. A resonance was set up, so to speak. From a distance, what one saw was a play of light and colour, dazzling but enjoyable. From within the structure itself . . .

Indescribable. But so devastating, his subconscious had undermined his long-standing plan to accustom himself to it slowly, returning day after day and each time witnessing the Flash from a closer spot until he was able to re-enter the mandala and comprehend what the sunlight was doing. Until today he had nearly forgotten he had ever so intended.

A hundred times, as he walked at her side, he formed the question on his lips: "Are you the Morag Feng who . . . ?"

And a hundred times, he abandoned it, afraid.

As when Marc had wandered off, most of the sightseers were congregated around the far side of the ship. She led him straight up to its hull, and through it. He winced as he entered. He had been so long here on Yan, he had almost forgotten about interpenetration doors. There was a corridor beyond, plain and white like the hull, elegantly proportioned but featureless.

"Gregory!" Morag said to the air.

The air answered. "Mr Chart is engaged with the Yanfolk still. However, it is projected that he will only be in conference for another four to six minutes. Phrases associated with leave-taking have been detected in the conversation."

"Fine. Then take us up to the main gallery, will you?"

The corridor instantly became an ascensor, and Marc felt the disturbing tug of a transversal gravity field. He was impressed. The equipment of this vessel was fantastic.

"Was that the—uh—the ship you were talking to?" he ventured after a moment.

"Hm? Oh, yes. Of course, Gregory had it specially built on Tubalcain."

Another few seconds, and they emerged on to a silver-railed gallery overlooking the huge central volume of the ship—although that was a mere fraction of its total bulk, the rest doubtless being taken up with the drive, the life-support systems, and the machinery required by Chart's profession. On the floor below, beyond a swirling one-way sound and vision screen, Marc saw a perfect simulation of a Yannish mansion-hall, in which a human—logically, Chart—sat talking with . . .

Marc blinked in amazement. He had fully intended to gaze fixedly at Chart, taking the greatest possible advantage of his first sight of this galaxy-famous artist who made him feel small, terribly young, and more than somewhat frightened.

But Chart wasn't just talking to "a Yannish delegation".

He was talking to the Yannish delegation. He was talking to Speaker Kaydad, and to Vetcho, and to Goydel. Marc would have recognised them anywhere.

Morag did something he didn't see, and voices came to his ears: Chart, and Kaydad, exchanging compliments as the visitors rose. It was a long moment before he realised that the words were in Yannish.

"Does Chart *speak* Yannish?" he demanded.

"That? Oh, of course not!" Morag answered impatiently. "The ship translates for him." She relented slightly, and turned her burning gaze directly on him. "Much of the vocabulary bank was primed from your translations," she said. "You should be proud."

Then, about three or four minutes later, she said, "Okay, they're on their way. Take us down."

With a stomach-churning lurch—which was actually perfectly smooth, only Marc was not prepared for it—the entire gallery descended to the main floor. The vision of the Yannish mansion dissolved at the same time, as Chart was escorting his visitors to the door, and by the time he turned back and noticed that Marc and Morag were present, it had turned into a pleasant glade carpeted with highly convincing grass and ringed with trees.

"You must be Marc Simon."

An—*ordinary* voice. Not quite the echoing, god-like thunder he had been half-imagining. He found himself offering his hand in return for Chart's, found himself establishing that the great man's grip was bony and rather weak, that his smile was skeletal and his whole body was thin to the point of being scrawny.

But a fire blazed behind his eyes. The second Marc met his gaze, he knew why this man was great.

A caress on Morag's bare forearm, and then: "Sit down! Some refreshment! Morag no doubt told you, this is a great pleasure for me, that I've long been looking forward to!"

Chairs sprang from nowhere, rustic in style to match the glade, and a table with a jug of chilled wine and several mugs.

"Hah! Good to be back in a chair—those Yannish cushions must take getting used to." Chart dropped his bony frame into one and gestured; the wine poured itself, and a full mug soared to within easy reach of Marc's hand. Morag chose a seat a little to one side, as though preferring to be audience at this encounter. A faint smile played around her lips.

"Your health," Chart said, seizing a mug which had risen before him in similar manner. "To the man with the greatest grasp of Yannish culture!" He drank, set the mug down, wiped his mouth with the back of his hand. "What *is shrimashey*, by the way?"

It was all going too quickly for Marc to follow, accustomed as he had been for years to the leisurely pace of Yannish society. Morag put her hand on Chart's shoulder.

"You're rushing him!" she exclaimed, and added to Marc, "You'll have to forgive him—he says he's always like this when a project really grabs hold of his imagination."

"True, true!" Chart gave a chuckle. "Yes, I'm sorry— I must appear a bit overwhelming in this state. Never mind! Can you tell me? It's what I most need to know."

"Well, it's—uh—it's primarily a population-balancing mechanism," Marc said after a pause. "But you must have heard about that."

"Oh, of course! I have kilometres, lightyears, parsecs of tape about it!" Chart gestured, and part of the surrounding glade faded away in favour of a display of *shrimashey* in progress in the open air, a satellite view of one of the rare public outbreaks which occurred perhaps once in ten or fifteen years and involved half the population of a town. Marc had seen this particular recording before, and it made his spine crawl now as it had done the first time: the sight of those masses of adult, mature Yanfolk piling into a writhing heaving confusion of bodies.

There had been eight deaths on that occasion.

"Everyone can find out that after a birth," Chart said, "the adult Yanfolk meet in groups and drink this—this drug which turns off their higher rational faculties, turning over their physical responses to the lower ganglion in the spine. That's the same one which is involved in sexual contact, right?"

Sexual contact . . .

Abruptly the entire story of Morag Feng sprang into Marc's memory. He had heard it once, barely paid attention . . . but now it came back with a crash. He said faintly, "Ah—yes!"

And wondered whether news of her return had yet reached Alice Ming.

"You'll forgive me, I hope," Chart murmured, "but in view of the—ah—the fact that you live with a Yannish girl I'd like to ask about this compatibility we have."

Hot words boiled to Marc's lips, but Morag forestalled what he would have said. She leaned forward and smiled.

"Gregory has heard all about it from a woman's point of view, Marc. He'd like to ask a man, as well."

Defeated, Marc leaned back in his chair, offered his mug to the jug for a refill and received it automatically, and said, "Well, you probably know that there's this organ, the *caverna veneris,* and when it's put in contact with the male proboscis it begins to throb, and massages these little flakes of skin off it. Which is what fertilises the female, only it's highly inefficient because the incidence of pregnancy averages twice a lifetime for a Yannish female, and they're sexually active from about age twenty-four to age one hundred thirty-five. It's not the same as it is with us, in that there's not the same element of tension in it, and there's no actual orgasm, no climax, but it's tremendously—uh—pleasurable for them, and so they like to do a lot of it. And there's this strong emotional commitment involved. Not like making love together among humans. More like—uh—agreeing to make a trip to another planet together. Something like that. A—a commitment." He gulped more wine.

"And the male has this same—what did you call it?—this same throbbing reflex," Chart pursued. "I see. And this is controlled by the corresponding lower spinal ganglion, the same which is activated during *shrimashey,* and . . . And it's gratifying to a human?"

There was something repulsive in Chart's tone, as though he were a voyeur, perverted. His voice sounded dirty. Mac was on the verge of a heated retort—though he could never have explained in a single sentence just what it was he felt about having Shyalee as a mistress, all the overtones of flattery, of determination to bridge inter-stellar gulfs as perhaps in the long-ago Dark Ages a few brave individuals had tried to bridge the gap between races and language-groups—when Morag said sharply, "Yes!"

And he had to admit the same was true for a man, and meekly echoed her.

"But no climax," Chart mused. "Does that mean there's some truth in the notion that *shrimashey* itself is a sort of orgasm—an instant discharge of neurotic and antisocial tendencies?"

Marc recovered abruptly from the distaste Chart's previous remark had evoked in him, and felt a stab of respect. If he was aware of that notion, he must have dug very deep indeed into the corpus of data human investigators had accumulated about the Yanfolk.

"There is a theory to that effect," Marc said after a pause to sip his wine. "I'm inclined to it myself. One knows that human orgasm does discharge tension. One would expect a similar need in the Yanfolk. What one finds is . . ." He spread his hands.

"Catharsis instead," Chart proposed.

"Well put! Yes, 'catharsis' is the nearest any human language has come to a concept relating to *shri-mashey*."

"And it works," Chart murmured.

"Something works," parried Marc. "At any rate, their—"

"Their society has been stable for millennia," Chart cut in. "I heard about that. But what interests me most of all is— Did you know a census had been conducted on Yan regularly for the past century?"

"What?" Marc stared at him. "But the Yanfolk . . ."

Oh. Not by them. By us.

"I see you caught on quickly," Chart smiled. "Yes, we have carried out a regular census ever since first contact. Did you know there are *always* one point eight times ten to the seventh Yanfolk, and there has never, in the past century, been a deviation from this figure amounting to more than *five*?"

Marc re-heard the words in recent memory . . . and jolted so violently he spilled his wine over his hand. He said hoarsely, "It can't be that exact!"

"The census?" Chart said.

"No, the . . . The population-control mechanism." Marc felt his eyes forced out to staring roundness.

"Apparently it is." That was Morag. "When I left here—you knew I'd been here before? Yes, I can read in your face that you did—when I left here, I determined to find out everything that was known about Yan, down to the things which Earthsider bureaucrats are so scared by that they're keeping them secret. I lost count of the men I had to seduce before I got what I wanted—though the experience stood me in good stead, you might say, because of Gregory."

Chart shared a wolfish grin with her, which paradoxically made him look older, not younger.

"Maybe it's because of the way I've always worked," he said now, "in that I've always exploited the latest technical advances—like this ship, which they built for me on Tubalcain to replace my former vessel—for artistic ends. But I seem, with guidance from Morag, to have detected a number of otherwise unnoticed patterns in Yannish culture. The precision with which *shrimashey* controls the population is known, of course, to the Earthsiders who thought of making census counts. They've done nothing with the data, though, except record them. I'm fascinated with a sexual reflex which incorporates a population-control technique of such precision. I'm fascinated by the existence of a drug which facilitates this *shrimashey*. This is the legacy, for me, of the so-called dramaturges. The Mutine Flash, the Mullom Wat, the Gladen Menhirs—they're static objects, aren't they? But this is a process, built in to the adult members of a numerous species, operating over millennia! And another thing! The Mutine Epics which you have so admirably translated!"

"What about them?" Marc forced out.

"How many books of them are there?"

"Why—why, eleven!"

"I think there are twelve," Chart said with deliberation. "I think I've spotted something you—with respect—overlooked. They are not just poems, they are a *technical manual*, and all that is missing is the key."

XII

MARC SAID EVENTUALLY, "I don't think I quite understand."

"Alchemy," Chart said. "Are you familiar with the magical and alchemical manuals they wrote on Earth some fifteen hundred years ago?"

The implications behind the words, of course, was: *I am*. With genuine humility, Marc admitted that he was not.

"I had to look into them last time I was hired by the continent of Europe." Chart drained his mug and let the jug refill it. His manner was lazy, casual, off-hand, that of a man with supreme and unchallengeable competence. "They were composed in a sort of association-code, using agreed conventional images—dragons, astrological figures, various oblique references of that kind. Provided one had been trained in the jargon, one could read them with relative ease. Outsiders, however, found only obscure and baffling nonsense. As a matter of fact, I'm astonished that you yourself aren't grounded in that area. Nothing I've run across, apart from those alchemical manuals, remotely resembles your rendering of the Mutine Epics."

"But the version you have," Marc hastened to point out, "is terrible! I was so proud of it a few years ago—and now I realise just what its shortcomings are."

"Can you rectify them?" Chart demanded.

"I . . ." Marc licked his lips. "Some of them," he said at length.

"Good. As you've no doubt gathered, this ship is equipped with one of the most superb computers ever designed, a late model from Tubalcain with approximately sixteen megabrains' capacity. Three or four times what you need to run a go-board, for example. Currently I have the two versions of the Mutine Epics—the translation you made, and the facsimile of the original which you deposited with the university that published it—running as a sub-programme, for reconciliation and comparison with all the alchemical manuals I've been able to locate. So far there's a high degree of concordance in that subtlest of attributes, style. I put it to you that the dramaturges of Yan, the so-called 'great scientists' of this planet, were nothing of the kind, but aesthetically biased. In a word, they were artists."

"Strangely enough," Marc said after a moment, "I'd been thinking just before Morag found me that you were the nearest human being I'd ever heard of to the Yannish dramaturges."

"Interesting!" Chart raised his eyebrows. "Because it's a parallel which had not escaped me." He spoke without false modesty. "Even through the filter of this translation which you now deprecate, I sensed a certain *rapport*."

"But this—this notion of the Epics as a technical manual," Marc said, reverting to the point which had sunk deep into his mind and begun to fester there, "is . . . Well, an interesting hypothesis, of course. What evidence have you for it, though?"

"I think I'll ask the ship for an opinion," Chart said with a shrug. "It's been analysing the content of the conversation I just had with Kaydad, Goydel and Vetcho." He checked. "Before I consult it, one more point. Am I correct in thinking that the Yanfolk would have selected their most—most conservative individuals to deal with us Earthsiders? I hinted as much to the computer."

"Oh, definitely," Marc declared. "There's an image which I've heard used, which perhaps ordinary people living in the enclave might not have run across. They talk as though the structure of their society were a tower, like the Mullom Wat, which has just that degree of flexibility needed to endure storms without resisting them. And the peak of the tower, the bit which sways furthest of all, is the bit which has to be of the finest workmanship."

"I see." Chart rubbed his chin. "The Mullom Wat, if I recall aright, is *the* one of the ancient artefacts which we would be hard put to it to duplicate?"

"Oh yes!" Marc was beginning to be caught up in the discussion now; he leaned forward with his elbows on his knees. "That's even more amazing than the Mutine Mandala: a single ovoidal column in the middle of the Ocean of Scand, one piece a hundred and thirty metres long, sunk through twenty metres of water into fifteen metres of bedrock and ooze. You've probably heard that the engineers attached to the first expedition, the discoverers of Yan, tried to think of a way of imitating it, and short of firing it vertically downwards there isn't one. Besides, there's no sign of violence around the foundation, and the material it's made from, a ceramic like porcelain, couldn't have stood the shock anyhow."

"I've heard about that, yes," Chart nodded. "But it doesn't do anything, does it? I mean, not in the sense that the Mutine Mandala does."

"Well, in high winds it does sing, like any openended pipe," Marc said. "But that's all." He hesitated, glancing at Morag. "By the way, I have to admit that I didn't place Morag's name when we met—not immediately."

She gave him a smile which didn't involve her eyes.

"I remember now, though. Weren't you the first person to experience the Mutine Flash from inside the Mandala?"

Her hand closed on her wine-mug so tightly that the knuckles showed paper-white. "I was," she said thinly after a tense pause. "Am I not still the only one?"

"I tried it," Marc said.

"Did you now? And—?"

"I went insane," Marc muttered, looking down into his own mug. "Afterwards, I promised myself I'd gradually work my way back to it. And I never have. I don't even make a point of seeing it every day."

"This Flash," Chart said. "Morag has told me about it, obviously. I gather it's unique—I mean, as a manifestation of function—among the ancient relics. What do you think it is?"

"I know only what the Epics say it is," Marc countered.

"Yes," Chart sighed. "They say it's the total information concerning their skills which the dramaturges enshrined in pillars of crystal, a sort of recording which the sun would daily replay until the end of the world. You believe that?"

"I think I do," Marc said. "Only I'm not sure that any human could ever understand the mode of communication employed. I suspect you'd need to have the Yannish lower ganglion, the one which is turned loose by the *sheyashrim* drug, to absorb those data."

"But the Yanfolk don't pay attention to their relics!" Morag broke in. "Do they?"

"True," Marc conceded. "Oh, you see children going to look them over now and then, but adults generally don't make a point of bothering. Even if they're on a journey to a far-distant city, which they've never made before, and it's taking weeks, they won't trouble to make a five-kilometre detour and visit a relic on the way."

"Do you really think it's the lack of a lower ganglion of Yannish type which prevents a human from absorbing the Mutine message?" Chart said. "Or do you think it's because the dust from the Ring garbles the solar spectrum?"

Marc stared at him for long moments. He said at last, "I—I wish I'd thought of that! It makes sense! Can it be tested?"

"Of course it can. I'm already testing it. Or, to be exact, I shall be with effect from tomorrow noon. If the Yanfolk never bother to go near their relics, they presumably won't mind my parking a remote sensor inside the Mandala, feeding back to my computer here. What it will do is simple: it'll record the Flash, for days on end, looking for the high peaks, the signal hidden in the noise, and then filter the noise out. Eventually, with luck, I shall be able to duplicate the Mandala here inside the ship, and use a simulated solar spectrum to—ah—'replay' the message."

"Fantastic!" Marc exclaimed.

"You approve?"

"Do I approve?" Marc was almost jigging up and down with excitement. "Why, it'd be wonderful . . ." His voice trailed away abruptly. "Is *that* what you meant when you said there was a twelfth book of the Mutine Epics?"

Chart gave a skeletal grin. "Well, of course. The Mandala itself, under everybody's noses for countless generations."

"The initiates' vocabulary," Morag said. "The key."

"Did you put him on to this idea?" Marc demanded of her. He was prepared, on the basis of this astonishing insight, to forget everything bad he had ever been told about her. At second-hand, he had never formed a really clear impression of the reasons why she had been so cordially disliked in the enclave during her former visit to Yan, and since he personally had no special fondness for the enclave and its people he was all the readier to discount what he had heard.

"I think I helped Gregory towards his conclusion," Morag said. "But mainly it's due to his background, his unique pattern of mentation. Do you know much about Gregory's work?"

Marc hesitated. "Not much. I mean, apart from Hyrax."

"That again!" Chart spoke with a tinge of disgust. "As though liberating a bunch of serfs were my sole justification for existing! I find it debasing—almost humiliating! Your Dr Lem, for example, only a short while ago, threw my work on Hyrax in my face, and I told him what I think of it, and I'm sure he didn't pay the least attention. Now listen, young man! You're a poet! If you can't understand my philosophy and my methods, then no one can!"

He hunched forward, while Marc prepared himself to listen with maximal attention. He could scarcely believe that he was really here, in Gregory Chart's ship, being lectured by the great man himself about his art.

And all of a sudden Chart had come alive. The fire behind his eyes spread, as though a gale had picked up a tiny flame and infected a whole forest. His voice crackled with it.

"You will grant, I trust, that the greatest creative force ever to work among intelligent beings—of any species—is the one which makes a culture? *That* is the force before which we all have to bow: poets, musicians, dramatists, philosophers . . . The process which evolves, patiently, with endless refinement, the totality into which all else is absorbed: *that* is the masterpiece of masterpieces! And it's nothing to do with individuals, except insofar as the time may be ripe for a particular person with a particular gift to leave his imprint on the ephemeral, malleable, fluid constituents of the culture.

"Where are the indices of a culture? In its museums?

Never! They are in the nursery-rhymes the children are babbling, the culture-heroes they are taught to emulate, the slang phrases, the jokes which abstract the attitudes of the society into a quintessential distillate like—like the contents of a medical syringe!"

Marc spared a second to look at Morag. She was sitting statue-still, yet poised as though she would nod at any moment, expressing her vigorous agreement.

"And they're in the ideals the members of that culture set for themselves, in the habits people have, in the tastes they show, in the preferences no matter how petty which they display.

"Now, since the advent of the go-board, we are at liberty to roam from one to another of—how many is it? Almost a hundred planets! Ninety-one, I think, last time I checked." Chart gave a harsh laugh. "Culture? On a world where the first arrivals did no more than break ground, build a few huts and general public services, and wandered on because they hated the settlers, the people looking for a permanent home who followed them from a dozen separate worlds and kept treading on their toes? That's what I take care of. *I make cultures*. Or, at least, I remake them. I dramatise them. I make them vivid, comprehensible, direct to their inhabitants. Sometimes I've worked with ancient traditions, on Earth. They hired me twice in North America, and three times in Europe, and once each in Asia, Africa, Australia. Then they wanted me for South America, and I decided not to accept. I moved on—to Cinula, Hyrax, Groseille, Logres, Pe t'Shwé! And in each place I analysed, studied, deduced, selected, taking those jokes, those nursery-rhymes, those garbled folk-memories, those tales and ballads and epigrams and—and *symbols* which form the shared experience of tens of millions of people. Is there a human culture in this galaxy? If there is, then *I built it*!"

Marc's throat was dry and his palms were prickly

with sweat. He could not have challenged that proud
assertion if his life had hung on doing so.

"You see? I am now one hundred and forty-five
years old. I have performed at least once for every human world. The last, and greatest, of my human chal-
lenges came on Tubalcain, where they paid me—in
part—by building this ship. To make a human culture
on a world which is so completely ruled by machines
that there is literally nothing except a child which is
manufactured without intervention of those machines,
not even air, not even drinking-water, not even food
. . . And I did it. Not with this ship, either. With my
old one, which I had used for half a century. And with
my own brain."

He put his palms on his temples, fingers outstretched
so that they looked like horns rising from his skull.

"What—what did they receive on Tubalcain?" Marc
whispered.

"The sense of belonging to a human society," Chart
said. "What else? I did what I always do—I drama-
tised. Have you woken in the morning to . . . ? Oh! I
don't know who your heroes are! But to a hero, who
greeted you and enlisted you in the venture which made
him that hero! To the company of conquerors who
gave your planet to you, who welcomed you as one of
their number and let you contribute to their great famous victory! Once, in Asia, I gave that sense of par-
ticipation, in a single month, to a hundred and eighty-
eight million people! But then, of course"—his voice
fell to a conversational level—"Earth is so unbelievably
rich."

Morag smiled and leaned back in her chair, as
though she had been worried about Chart's ability to
summarise his work adequately, but was now well satisfied with his explanation.

"Ten thousand years from now," Chart said, "they
will recognise me as the binding force in human space
colonisation. It would have been a good point at which

to stop. Unfortunately I am still healthy and active and have no desire to stop. Had it not been for falling in with Moràg, I might have lapsed into suicidal despair. But she did seek me out and suggest to me . . . Yan."

He folded his hands comfortably on his lap. "They tell me that without being human the Yanfolk are amazingly close to us Earthsiders. Splendid. They have a culture which is rocking under the gentle, barely noticeable impact of the little human enclave here. Do they require it to be bolstered, re-dramatised for its members after so many millennia during which their nourishment has been no more than folklore, ancient legends, thin and watery fare? Well, do they? I was about to ask the ship, a short time ago, precisely that question. It must by now have completed the analysis of the conversation it recorded during the visit by the Yannish delegation."

Marc tensed. From the air, the same voice he had heard when Morag brought him on board said, "Analysis confirms the tentative prediction. Aware that their culture is vulnerable to the superior material achievements of mankind, the *hrath* in-group of the Yanfolk have been desperately hunting for means to re-actualise the great days of the past and thereby counter the so-called 'aping' of human behaviour by the younger generation. Having totally failed despite their best efforts, they are now prepared to adopt any means which comes to hand. Their fullest assistance will be forthcoming."

"Might I also hope," Chart said when that had sunk in, "for the assistance of the greatest living translator of Yannish poetry? I think I shall need it; machines—as I learned the hard way on Tubalcain—leave a great deal to be desired."

Marc sat rigid for long moments, his brain whirling. On the one hand, the risk of deranging Yannish society, so stable for so long, by applying human bias to its cherished ancient dreams; on the other, the tempting prospect of being associated with the first ever of

Chart's performances to be built around an alien tradition.

And if Chart is right, and he really knows how to recover the key which will turn the Mutine Epics into a technical manual . . .

He said suddenly, not quite having taken the decision, "Yes, of course!"

XIII

"A—A MESSAGE, Warden," Erik Svitra said nervously as he crossed the living-area of the Chevsky home. Somehow, since the moment when the warden spotted him and swept him up in his wake, returning to the enclave from the spot where Chart's ship rested, he seemed to have become—well—*involved*. There was an old-fashioned aura of politicking which informed this house; people came and went all day, and its owner sat holding court among them. Erik had conceived the blasphemous notion that a man bearing the only official, Earth-granted title in the enclave ought to get out and around a bit more, ought to feel the pulse of his community more directly. But he was a stranger, and on this alien-dominated world perhaps things operated differently.

Interrupting his conversation with the Dellian Smiths, Chevsky said, "What message? What about?"

"It's printed for you only," Erik said, and held out the small autosealed capsule which the communet had just delivered. That was a facility rare on more advanced worlds; he had wondered ever since his first day on Yan just what the purpose was of according such elaborate facilities to such a small and relatively poor community of humans.

"Excuse me," Chevsky muttered, and thumbed the capsule. It hesitated a fraction of a second before identifying him, then split with a pop and unreeled its contents. He scanned them.

"Well, I'll be . . . The bitch! The *bitch!*"

The Smiths stared at him, and Erik, and the other people in the room: nine of them. Erik had learned some of their names, but ever since that encounter with the *gifmak* drug his memory had had lacunae in it.

"Sid!" Chevsky said with magnificent disgust. "Hell, it's a plot, that's what it is! They're out to get me!"

"Who?" demanded Smith's wife, Rachel.

"Lem—and Pokorod—and Ducci—and the rest of that self-appointed gang of self-important bastards!" Chevsky rolled the message and capsule into a ball and hurled it at a disposer. "Know what they've done now?"

Heads shook on all sides of him.

"Sid's gone. Took a go-board route this morning and went without even talking to me!" Huge exaggerated tears formed in Chevsky's eyes, and Rachel handed him tissues to wipe them.

"She wasn't much!" he forced out through sudden sobs. "But she was a wife for me, and a man needs a wife!"

Heads nodded, just as they had shaken.

"Without even saying goodbye!" Chevsky burbled.

I wonder how she swung that deal, Erik thought. *I guess she must have had private credit stacked up. He'd insist on controlling their joint account. Lucky bitch! I wish I could afford a go-board route!*

"That settles it, then!" Chevsky roared. "We call a town's meeting on this! Put in a majority petition to Earth, get rid of those pompous bastards! I mean we want to see Chart perform here, right?"

"Right!"—in a chorus.

"Even if it's a performance based on the—the native

traditions, not ours!" Chevsky put out his hand and someone thrust a full glass into it, some sort of beer. Erik had sampled it and found it sour.

He was fairly certain he knew who had fed Chevsky that line. Rachel Smith was possessed of a certain naïve subtlety—if that were possible—and knew how to sugar unpalatable facts. He detected her influence in the next remarks, as well.

"After all, perhaps the great skill of this famous artist Gregory Chart will help us to understand our native neighbours better, ease our adjustment of life-patterns!"

Not that the notion registered well with everyone . . .

"In any case, though," Chevsky pursued relentlessly, "we've been fortunate in that Erik over there *not* only helped me—uh—save my face when my bitch of a wife wanted to screw me up . . ."

Pause. Several grins aimed at Erik, who stood there hating it but trying, from politeness, to grin back.

"*But* also tipped off a news-machine which had heard about Chart—and dashed for the go-board—and went into TE mode before Ducci and that meddling son of his could stop it." Chevsky leaned back expansively, stretching his arms and legs. "Thanks to which . . . I guess I didn't tell you before, but I just made some inquiries through the informat, and that news-machine was registered on *Earth*. So we can rely on the news about Chart having spread throughout the inhabited galaxy."

Pause. To let the statement sink in.

"Which means that we are going to be put well and truly on the map. According to the informat, wherever Chart goes a gang of wealthy tourists from Cinula, Ilium, Groseille, and even Earth go too, in order to catch his latest masterwork. The first time he hits an alien-type culture, they expect to like double the mass interest he regularly gets. Here's the biggest commercial proposition ever on Yan, isn't it?"

"I don't see Pedro Phillips here," said a voice from the corner of the room furthest from Erik. The speaker was someone Erik didn't really know, had only heard the name of, a certain Boris Dooley who had apparently wandered off the board a few years ago and stopped over longer than he meant to. He worked at reclamation and purification along with the Smiths.

Chevsky favoured him with a scowl. "Meaning—?" he invited, his voice taking on a dangerous purr.

"Meaning Pedro's the merchant of the enclave," Boris said. "Meaning if there were real commercial interest in the matter he'd be on our side. I want to know why Doc Lem, and Doc Pokorod, and the rest, are scared by Chart."

There was a short hostile silence. Erik said suddenly, not having intended to speak up, "I . . ."

All eyes fixed on him. He licked his lips.

"Well!" he said obstinately. "I mean I know *I* just dropped in here the other day. I mean I don't have too much say in this matter. But I have been around—like I made it to over thirty worlds already, in my professional capacity—and I do get this bad feeling about Chart, who's an Earthsider, taking on this big ancient Yannish scene. I mean, like, there are things out there we couldn't duplicate, right? I mean there are some of these Yan people who don't like humans. I mean . . ."

He spread his plump brown hands helplessly. "I mean I can feel like something *bad*," he concluded. "Last place I want to be when Chart cuts loose is right on the same planet. And that's my carefully considered opinion."

He could tell, just by looking, he had touched a sore spot in the minds of several of the people in the room. But Chevsky said bluffly, "Now look here, Erik, feller! You only just got here, you said so yourself! You leave the worrying to us, hm? You just enjoy your first stopover in Yan—or get back on the go-board if you don't like it. Leave the worrying to us old hands. *We* know what to do about all this!"

"Sorry," Erik muttered, and moved to take a chair in an obscure corner.

"Right!" Chevsky went on. "We were talking about calling a town's meeting, weren't we? Anyone here feel it's not necessary?"

No one.

"Good, then we can push ahead. I guess it wouldn't be an exaggeration to say that we have right now and right here in this room an influential cross-section of the humans on Yan, and if we play our cards right we should be able to swing the meeting around to . . ."

Erik stopped listening. He was calculating whether his surviving credit would stake him to a go-board course for another world. Not necessarily a world where he could hope for good pickings in his trade— just somewhere other than Yan.

He could feel his spine crawl every time anyone mentioned Chart performing for these here alien natives. He had long ago acquired a healthy respect for the prickly premonitions he now and then experienced. The way he saw it, the best viewpoint during a Chart performance was from any other world bar the one where he was currently in business.

Of course, it would be a shame to leave Yan without having tried out this reputed sexual compatibility bit. But . . . !

Great artist! What does that not excuse? Hell! Like novaing a sun to study the effect of a sudden rise in temperature on the culture of its habitable planet!

At approximately the same moment:

"Is there any means whereby we can constitute ourselves a legal entity?" worried Pedro Phillips. As a merchant, he was involved in interstellar trade, and owing to the risk of spreading disease, or unstabling precarious local economies, there were many many regulations he had to take into account. It followed that he would be the one preoccupied by legalisms.

It seemed equally fitting that Ducci should be the one to snort, and to say with force, "Legal? Legal precedents don't happen until the first time—and what we have here is a first time, isn't it?"

Around him, in comfortable chairs on Dr Lem's verandah overlooking his famous i hedge, precisely that group which he had long thought of as "responsible" in the enclave—whether or not they had authority—exchanged sober looks and nods. At her master's feet, Pompy uttered a sigh. Like all chubbles she was sensitive to the mood of those around her owing to the vast olfactory zones on her back, and she was beginning to get annoyed with the continual crises she could detect through the stench of tension which assailed her. Last night, Dr Lem recalled, she had had a nightmare. That was the first since their arrival on Yan. She had clawed and scrabbled into bits a valuable Yannish rug.

This egocentric bastard Chart! Stirring us around like a pot of stew!

He said, hoping to introduce a calmer note, "Let's review what we so far know. Let's—"

"What is there to reconsider?" interrupted the normally calm Jack Shigaraku. He hunched forward on his chair. "We know Chart has received a favourable response, not only from the young apes, but from the conservative older Yanfolk. We know he's enlisted the help of Marc Simon, and whether or not one approves of his behaviour"—letting it be implied that he didn't, which was not surprising, because like all tutors on foreign worlds he had an acute sense of the continuity of Earthsider culture and wanted it to be preserved—"one must compute with the fact that he has the greatest understanding of Yannish of any living human. He's turned his coat, so to speak. He's . . ."

He cancelled the conclusion of the sentence, and sat

back. But it was clear, Dr Lem realised, that everyone knew what he had been going to say.

"If only it hadn't been Morag Feng who lured Chart here!" Jack's wife Toshi mourned.

"But it was," Pedro snapped. "And we're stuck with the fact!" Having seized their attention, he continued: "As to making ourselves a legal entity, I've been consulting the informat and—"

The communet sounded. Dr Lem turned in his chair with a muttered apology, and as he reached for the floating extension which served the verandah heard Pedro doggedly ploughing on: "And I find that we, as a quorum of the total human population, have the right to declare ourselves a political entity. A—hell, what's the word? Oh, yes, a *party!* What we have to do now is this. When the next town's meeting is called . . ."

He suddenly grew aware that no one was listening to him. Everybody else had turned to stare at Dr Lem, and at the miniature communet screen which had drifted toward his chair. The image on it was poor, and the sound was almost as bad as it squawked and blasted from the speaker. But the characteristics were unmistakable.

"That's an interstellar call!" Toshi said in a tone of awe, and added unnecessarily, "Shhh!"

From the screen the shifting, blurred, but occasionally identifiable image of a plump but quite attractive woman with dark hair and bright pink cheeks was saying: "Dr Lem! One finds you in the directory for the enclave on Yan as its doyen, the only person listed except the warden who is currently not taking calls, so you'll forgive me if—"

"Who are you?" Dr Lem interrupted, recovering from his surprise. "Where are you calling from? What do you want?"

"My name is Claudine Shah, and I'm calling from Earth," the woman said. Everyone on the verandah tensed. A call from Earth! There could have been no more than half a dozen of those since the foundation of the enclave.

"And I represent a travel bureau which has long been considering the addition of a ringed world to its available itineraries. A news-machine that passed your way recently reported the presence of Gregory Chart on Yan, and obviously this would be an optimum chance to—"

"Cancel this call," Dr Lem said. The screen obediently blanked. He let the 'net extension drift away from him with a lax hand and turned to look at his companions.

None of them spoke.

"I propose," Dr Lem said finally, "that we file petition with the government of Earth as a responsible pressure-group—what's the word? Ah! A *lobby!* To have Chart removed from Yan, if necessary by force. Something has got to be done to stop him re-creating the Mutine Age!"

XIV

"So now I have my first chance to see this famous Mutine Flash," Chart murmured, bringing the high-speed floater to a hover. Marc had not ridden in one of these for years, and never in such an advanced model: totally soundless, not betraying by the least quiver or vibration that it was moving. No doubt this too was part of the payment Chart had exacted from Tubalcain.

The sun was just starting to tint the crystal shafts of the Mandala now. Chart had timed their arrival perfectly.

"Have you planted your detector?" Marc asked.

"Oh, yes." Chart squinted sidewise at the haloed sun. "But don't expect quick results, will you? It may take a score, perhaps a hundred superposed recordings before the signal can be extracted from the noise. That blur of dust around the sun must muddle the spectrum terribly."

"Here it comes!" Morag said from the rear seat of the vehicle.

Down the translucent pillars a kind of fire suddenly washed: the sum and epitome of everything men had ever admired in a well-cut jewel. Pure colours shone

out like the boom of a bell, were thrust aside by others
in bands, in stripes, in swirling curves. Pearly irides-
cence overlaid one upon another, and then they dissolved together into new hues, while the light behind
them grew unbearably brilliant. Yet they could not tear
their eyes away. For Marc—doubtless also for
Morag—there were hurtful memories being awoken; no
modern man or woman could enjoy remembering that
he or she had gone insane.

Tantalisingly, a hint of meaning, of significance, rode
the waves of colour, as though one were to chance on a
worn rock half-buried in the ground and discern that
there had once been an inscription on it, but in an al-
phabet whose last user was dead a thousand years.

A brief incredible dazzling tumult of visual glory—
and it was over. The sun was past the zenith.

Chart exhaled loudly. Marc suspected he had held
his breath throughout the thirty-six seconds of the
Flash. Now he said in a tone of awe, "So much! And in
so short a time! Why, it makes my little tricks with the
aurora look like a—a baby's finger-painting!"

"You said it," Morag murmured. "I don't think you
believed me really, did you? Until now!"

"I . . ." Chart sat back in his control-chair. "I guess
I didn't. And these Yanfolk don't even bother to come
and watch that?"

"I've never known any adult to come and watch it,"
Marc confirmed.

"Fantastic!" Seeming almost dazed, Chart shook his
head. "You know I create sensory nuclei to assist my
performances, don't you? Objects—constructs—which
radiate various signals, heighten mood, predispose the
public to the response I want . . . But I never contrived anything as spectacular as that!"

There was a short silence. Eventually he rubbed his
eyes and took the floater's controls again. "Where next?
Oh, yes. These things they call the Gladen Menhirs."

So: a complete survey of the relics. The Gladen

Menhirs marching in a perfect line around the entire planet, on land and under water; at intervals of precisely thirty-two point four kilometres: identical masses of synthetic stone, each sixty-seven metres high by fourteen square, with rounded corners. The Mullom Wat, rising from the Ocean of Scand, humming gently as the wind played across its open top. A vast empty volume cut into a monstrous rock, a kind of granite, with benches inside on which ten thousand Yanfolk might have sat in comfort, facing a blank wall. A spiral maze, like a seashell cut through the middle, leading in towards a central circle . . . and then out again. Going nowhere.

And onwards . . . It took a day and a night and a day to visit all the most important relics in the northern hemisphere alone; they ate while flying and slept during the traverse of the ocean, automatically woken twice in order to circle down over mysterious little isolated objects poking out of the water, not as remarkable as the Mullom Wat but equally enigmatic.

And, at each halt, Chart revealed how thoroughly he had studied Yan before setting course for it. As an appendix to his translation of the Epics, Marc had included a list of tentative identifications of these relics with items referred to in the poem. Some were not at all hard to recognize; the Mutine Mandala appeared so many times that there was no room for argument, and the Mullom Wat and a few others were almost as unmistakable. Where problems began to arise was when there was a chance that the original relic mentioned in the text no longer survived—had been located in Kralgak, perhaps, and smashed by the rain of meteorites.

But Chart kept saying, after he had inspected a certain object, "Could that be the monument described in Book Six, where they're turning the forest back through time?" Or else: "That reminds me of the passage near the beginning of Book Two where the dramaturges meet in council on a high headland."

Marc sat there, marvelling, and doing his best to confirm or deny these enlightened guesses. Time and again Chart seemed to spot, instantly, something he himself had overlooked. With every passing minute he found himself becoming more impressed.

And then, eventually, Chart said, "Right! Now for the southern hemisphere."

Marc stared at him for a long moment. He said at last, "In—in this thing? You mean straight across Kralgak?"

"Why not? I want to see the southern relics, too. And of course I must take a look at the wilders."

"But . . .!" Marc's objection died on his lips as he glanced around the interior of the floater. Yes, a late-model Tubalcain floater probably could traverse Kralgak unharmed.

"Worried about the meteorites?" Morag murmured. "No need! You don't think I'd let Gregory risk his life, do you? Or mine! It's rather precious to me."

"Uh . . . Yes, of course. I guess I've been conditioned by associating with the Yanfolk. For them, of course, the mere idea of crossing Kralgak is unthinkable."

"I expect it to be quite an impressive trip," Chart said. "But nothing short of a twenty-ton rock could even displace this floater from its course. We'll cross the ocean, though, rather than Kralgak proper. According to my sources, the densest concentration of wilders is to be found along the nearer shore of the southern continent, and from here we can fly a Great Circle course direct to where they live."

Despite his best intentions, when Marc saw the white foam on the deep blue water ahead, marking the limit of the zone where the meteorites pelted continually down, he had to brace himself, and his knuckles grew white on the arms of his seat. But Chart betrayed no tension—only a hint of excitement. Now and then he lifted an eyebrow to comment on an expecially large splash. The whole sky, as they drew closer, seemed to be threaded with irregular streaks of fire, and there was a faint jar and Marc glanced up in alarm to find that a pebble had smashed on the transparent canopy of the floater. And there beyond was the daylight shimmer of the Ring, just visible through the blue blur of the sky: a faint, faint white band—

Another pebble struck, and he winced. He heard Morag chuckle. Annoyed with himself, he turned his gaze downward, and there saw the water roiling and churning, exactly as though a fast current were pouring it over rapids.

But it was at its deepest here. The rocks nearest the surface must be a good hundred metres down.

"Magnificent," Chart said. "Absolutely magnificent."

And . . . Yes, in a way it is. Marc had to concede that. Not that it was compensation for losing half a planet.

"There!" Chart exclaimed suddenly, and threw up his arm towards the zenith. A vast lump of rock, weighing tons, was blasting downward to the right of their course, leaving a blinding stripe of white across the air. When it struck the water, there was a colossal explosion, and a fountain of steam shot hundreds of metres into the air. Wind caught the spray, and for a brief instant the canopy of the floater was smeared with wet, before the automatic cleansing mechanism restored it to perfect transparency.

"I wish I could get some really clear conception of the Yanfolk as they were in their great period," Chart muttered. "I have this fairly accurate picture of the dramaturges, I think, but it's the survivors I'm puzzled by. Marc!"

"Yes?"

"Marc, you know humans. Imagine some great disaster overtaking mankind back on Earth, before the go-board. Imagine—oh, say a war! You do know what a war is?"

"Yes."

"Or any other kind of major disaster which overwhelmed the contemporary version of civilisation. Could you believe in mankind being so disheartened that they abandoned all hope of reconstruction?"

"I—I guess I could," Marc said. "But only if they were reduced to savagery, like the wilders."

"Yes, exactly. These wilders we're going to look at are typical of what might have happened to mankind, although even in that case I'd have expected them to begin again after a few centuries, not remain in apathetic barbarism for ten thousand years." The rain of fire continued on all sides, the ocean below seethed and surged, but he was no longer looking at it. "The civilized Yanfolk, though! Incredible! Relinquishing the—the *cream* of their achievements, as it were, and apparently being content with mere existence from that day forward."

"Not altogether content," Morag said from the rear.

"You mean these apes?" Chart said over his shoulder. "I know. There is discontent, that's plain enough. But it took contact with mankind to spark it, and what's a century compared to the previous nine and a half millennia? It's almost as though the dramaturges were a diffferent species, isn't it? The spearhead of the race, as you might say. A small group in which all initiative, originality, inventiveness had been concentrated, and when they disappeared . . . " A gesture like spilling sand from his palm. "Yet they were the same species, weren't they?"

"I don't know that anyone has ever suggested they were not," Marc said.

"And the wilders?"

"I've never seen any myself," Marc admitted. "But there are recordings you can dial from the informat.

Physically they're identical with the rest of the Yanfolk, except that they're sometimes stunted, or diseased."

"I see," Chart nodded. "Ah! Clearer water ahead. We must be through the meterorite zone."

Another pebble smashed on the canopy. But it made no more impression than the others. The floater continued unperturbed on its course.

They found a tribe of wilders within less than half an hour of encountering the coast of the southern continent. Chart had put the floater into the anti-see mode, and it was neither visible nor audible as it drifted gently down along the reddish sandy shore. There were about twenty or twenty-five in the tribe they discovered: all naked, except for garlands of leaves around their neck and waists, and about equally divided between men and women. They had two children with them, but these were both very young and being carried.

They were hunting for buried sand-worms, using sharpened sticks or their toes to rout the creatures out of their burrows. The moment they discovered them, they ate them. Only two of them carried them away from the spot where they were located; both these were men, who ran to the women carrying the children and handed over about half their spoils.

"Fathers?" Chart inquired.

"Not likely," Marc decided when he had thought about it for a moment. "I seem to recall something about this in the informat recordings. They take turns in providing for the children. It's a kind of rudimentary version of the northern pattern. You know that newborn children are dispatched in a special container called a *kortch* to a relative in another city, and may not see their natural parents again until they're five or six years old?"

"Of course. I studied up on Yannish familial relationships." Chart was peering down with concentration at the wilders. "Yes, they do look physically very much like the northerners. Let's see if we can hear them talking, shall we?"

He flipped a control. Marc could not see anything happening; he asked what it was for.

"I've sent out an anti-see monitor," Chart said. "And by the sound of it, there's not much talking going on, is there? Here!" He turned a knob, and there was a sudden soft sound in the cabin, the splash of wavelets on the beach, modified now and then by the brushing of feet among the low-lying liminal vegetation.

"And they have no weapons," he mused. "And only tools for crude jobs like digging. Correct?"

Marc nodded.

"I think they'll do fine," Chart declared suddenly. "But we'll have to make doubly certain, of course. Let's pick up that one who's wandered out of sight of the rest." He pointed with one hand to a male who had gone behind a large boulder, and with the other hand tapped a pattern of instructions on the control-board.

The man rose abruptly into the air, seeming to yell, and vanished.

"What are you doing?" Marc demanded.

"Just studying him, seeing if he's suitable," Chart answered absently. "Hmm! Yes, physically in fair shape—a bit undernourished, but that could be rectified . . . Oh, yes! These wilders will do very well, if he's a typical specimen."

"Do very well—for what?" Marc said slowly. A cold, unpleasant suspicion was burgeoning at the back of his mind.

"To be pithed and programmed, of course," Chart sighed. "I don't have facilities to make up Yannish androids, do I? It'd be hell's own job arranging for that, and expensive, too. But we've got to have programmed actors available, to take the dramaturge rôles when the performance gets under way."

"Now let me get this straight." Marc bit his lip.

"You're proposing to pith these wilders? To—to decorticate them?"

"I just told you!" Chart snapped. "We shall *have* to have programmed actors!"

There was a dead silence, apart from the clicking of the instruments which were continuing to analyse the bodily condition of the captive.

"Take me back to Prell," Marc said at last.

Chart stared at him.

"I said take me back to Prell," he repeated. "I won't have anything whatever to do with this!" He clenched his fists.

"Marc, be reasonable!" Morag said, sitting forward.

"You heard me!" Marc roared. "Come on! Put that poor devil back on the ground, and take me home!"

XV

WHAT ARE WE—*supplicants?*

Walking stiffly at the head of the little delegation, self-appointed, on the way to visit Speaker Kaydad, Dr Lem found the question recurring and recurring in his mind. At his side Hector Ducci marched with determined, heavy steps; the Shigarakus, Harriet and Pedro brought up the rear. One last hope remained, they agreed, before they turned to Earth for assistance which was unlikely to be forthcoming. An appeal to Chart was certain to fail; an appeal to Chevsky was absurd, because he had already convinced himself that to have Chart perform on Yan while he was warden of the enclave would make him famous, perhaps lead to him being transferred to a major post on another planet.

But an appeal to the Yanfolk might—just *might* . . .

"We're almost there, aren't we?" Toshi said from behind him. He nodded. They had passed the tenuous border between the human and the Yannish zones of Prell about five minutes ago. Now they were surrounded not by the cuboidal, dogmatic shapes of human architecture, but by the almost egg-like forms of Yannish homes, their flat open roofs hidden by curved upper walls, their exterior almost featureless because the focus of their layout was inward, centered on the atrium and the pool, or the flowerbeds, or the carvings, or whatever other items the owners had selected as particularly to their taste.

"Where is everybody?" Ducci muttered. "I never saw the streets so empty before!"

"Can't you smell?" Harriet answered. "They're making *sheyashrim*." She sniffed exaggeratedly.

"What?" Ducci copied her. "Why—why, yes! I hadn't noticed before, but I guess that's the third or fourth house we've passed where I could smell it."

"More like thirtieth or fortieth," Jack Shigaraku said sourly, quickening his stride for a moment and coming up alongside Ducci and Dr Lem. "They must be brewing it by the barrelful."

There was silence among them for a moment as they all thought of that potent drug being prepared in such colossal quantities. Ordinarily, it was only required for the day following a birth, when—as though by an impulse from the collective racial subconscious of the Yanfolk—it was drunk ceremoniously among groups of responsible adults, who thereupon lapsed into wild animal dancing and ultimately into a rioting mass of crushed-together bodies.

"Is this something to do with Chart's plan?" Toshi asked when they had gone another few paces. Her husband shook his head.

"I've no idea. Yigael?"

Dr Lem sighed. "According to Marc's translation of the Mutine Epics, the *sheyashrim* drug was developed by the dramaturges just prior to their great undertaking. But I'm afraid I've never read the Epics in the original. I can only take his word for it."

"That bastard!" Toshi said with venom. "Obsessed, that's what he is! Throwing his lot in with Chart, the way he has—doesn't he realise what he's helping to bring about?"

Dr Lem gave her a sidelong glare. He said, "Marc has never been kindly treated by the people of the enclave, has he? And you and Jack have been among those who treated him worst."

"Now just a moment—" Jack began.

"I mean it!" With uncharacteristic force Dr Lem tilted his head back and stared the tutor in the eyes. "I know you prize human culture, I know you're angry because he seemed to prefer Yannish company to that of his own kind. But he committed himself to his chosen course for a purpose. And before this is all over, I predict we're going to be grateful for his comprehension of Yannish. Let's face it! Without his translation of the Mutine Epics, what else would we have to tell us what's likely to happen?"

"Without it, would Chart have been attracted to Yan?" Jack snapped.

"If he had ever conceived the notion of performing for a non-human audience, he would have picked on Yan as a logical first choice," Dr Lem insisted.

"More to the point," Harriet put in, "it was Morag Feng who brought Chart here, not Marc. That's what we have to reckon with."

"Do you think she's here for revenge?" Pedro asked.

"No. For something far more dangerous. Justification for her own stupidity."

"There's Kaydad's house," Dr Lem said, pointing. "And they're expecting us." The gloglobe at its door was green, to show that an appointment had been made with distinguished visitors, and casual callers should return at another time.

Vetcho was with the Speaker, which was to be expected. So was Goydel, which was not. With the utmost in stiff formality they welcomed the visitors and seated them on the traditional Yannish cushions. The atrium here was unique, so far as Dr Lem knew, and he had never liked it. Instead of a pool in the centre, or a statue, or a flowering bush, it had a well, about four metres by two and at least twelve deep, with neither rails nor even a kerb around it.

He tried to look at the wall-hung tapestries instead, woven of coloured reeds.

But all was not as it should be. He detected that as soon as he entered, because the air was full of the scent of *sheyashrim,* and he knew the others had noticed it as well. And then the Speaker's matron offered, by way of refreshment, ghul-nut cordial.

It was delicious. But to a human it was poisonous. Even one cup induced stomach-cramps, and about three delirium.

A snub. A carefully weighed and deliberate snub.

The preliminaries took, for a group this size, around fifteen or twenty minutes. After that, when the matron withdrew, Kaydad should have broached the subject of his visitors' business in their own language—Yannish having been used up to that point, a standard courtesy.

He stuck to Yannish.

As you like, Dr Lem sighed inwardly, and hoped that his own rather shaky command of the language would not lead to misunderstandings.

"This is the planet of the Yanfolk, not of humans, and we have altered certain of our customs to accord with those of your people," he said. "There is a matter of considerable gravity to be discussed. So far as it is concerned, I am *Elgadrin.*" He employed the term normally rendered "Speaker".

"While one would not wish to cast doubt upon the assertion of one making such an important statement . . ." That was Vetcho. He'd been afraid it might be. Vetcho was notoriously far more conservative and chauvinistic than Kaydad.

"One would draw to present-time attention the existence of a person bearing a title, namely 'Warden'."

"The office held by Warden Chevsky relates to affairs in the human enclave, not to relationships between our two species. Routine administrative matters can be dealt with by him for convenience. The matter being discussed is not routine." Dr Lem wanted to wipe his face, but decided he should not do so. So far, though, he was making his points in good clear Yannish. If only he could keep up the standard . . .

He wished irrelevantly he hadn't had to leave Pompy at home. But the Yanfolk had never, seemingly, kept pets, and inviting an animal to join the company was a grave insult.

"That matter being . . . ?" Kaydad, now.

"The re-creation by Gregory Chart of the Mutine Age."

The humans tensed. They had been prepared for a far longer session of preamble. Dr Lem could tell from their deliberately calm faces that they were worried about the impact of this blunt statement.

Eventually Kaydad said, his face as frozen as a stone mask, "That matter is undebatable."

The word was far more forcible. It was in the philosophical negative mode, the mode of absolute denial reserved for such statements as universal categorical nulls.

"That it has no existence?" hazarded Dr Lem, groping among the shredded remains of his formal Yannish, which he had studied thoroughly during his first five or ten years on the planet, and lately neglected. "Or that it has no—uh—referents in speech?"

The two were clearly separable in this ancient, complex tongue.

"That it has no referents permitting argument," Goydel said. The others signified concurrence.

"In other words," Dr Lem said in his own language, "it's going to be done whether or not we approve."

Silence.

"I see," he went on eventually. "It has therefore come to this: that the once-proud Yanfolk have so far despaired of recapturing their ancient glory, they must hire a human to help them."

And waited. In memory he could hear Chart's mocking voice saying that because he had spent so long among the Yanfolk he had forgotten how to frame an insult. That might be true in his own speech. In Yannish, however, he obviously knew very well how to be rude. He had never seen any of the Yanfolk so furious before. Goydel was trembling, his hands curled into fists. Kaydad was working his mouth as though trying to speak, and failing. Only Vetcho had enough command of his own body to rise, and he, the moment he was on his feet, flung out his arm towards the street door.

"Go!" he ordered. "*Go!*"

"Get up slowly," Dr Lem muttered from the corner of his mouth. "Don't hurry. Move as though you don't give a damn for Yan or Yanfolk. Don't say goodbye, just leave."

The others, nervous, complied.

Rising himself, limbs stiff and awkward, Dr Lem said more loudly, "What a shame. When I first came here, I believed there to be a pride." It was more than pride; it was that, plus *amour propre,* plus self-respect, plus a sense of honour, plus, plus, plus . . . "One sees now that this cannot be supported unless an alien expert is hired to underpin it. A shame. A considerable disappointment. Perhaps one will go look for a more rewarding planet."

He had his back to the three Yanfolk by the time he concluded. Toshi and Harriet had passed through the exit, and Jack and Ducci were following. A hand fell on his thin shoulder. Perhaps it was the first time a Yannish hand had gripped a human in anger.

And in anger it certainly was. He was whipped around to confront Vetcho, dark eyes glazing in the pale mask-like upper portion of his face.

"Go or stay, as you wish!" he rasped. "You say we *hired* this human, this Gregory Chart? Deluded fool! We don't understand your notion of 'hiring', paying someone to do what he doesn't want! He came here to ask us for our help in planning something *he* desires to do! We have been pleased to grant it, because we have something you do not, something you never will have, and at long last one of you, one human, has recognised its genuine worth."

In the doorway Pedro and Ducci had paused, ready to free Dr Lem by force if need be.

But Vetcho dropped his hand, breathing hard.

"It may take a thousand years for you to understand what we are, what we learned how to do," he said. "Or you may never understand. Perhaps if you do you will not be so contemptuous, arrogant, overweening. We discovered our limitations long ago, and we decided to live within them. When, if ever, do you hope to achieve as much?"

He thrust Dr Lem through the door and slammed it behind him.

When they had gone fifty paces down the street Pedro cleared his throat.

"Oonagh and I," he said, referring to his wife, "have been thinking about getting ourselves a go-board pattern. So we can keep out of the way while this—this performance lasts. Put the store on auto, of course."

"It may last months," Dr Lem said.

"I know." Jack clenched his fists. "We've been thinking of closing the school, too—this will be no place for kids—but you can't make the parents understand. Chevsky and his pals got to most of them at once. Biggest event in the history of Yan, of course, your kids must witness it, something to talk about when they grow up!"

"We'll have to recommend it formally," Jack said. "Do you realise they're already playing *shrimashey*, those kids?"

Hector Ducci said bluffly, "Of course! I recall Zepp playing it, years ago!"

"It was all right when it was just an excuse for some body contact and mutual exploration," Toshi said. "But now they seem to feel the game doesn't come out right unless at least one kid winds up unconscious."

"I didn't know about that!" Ducci exclaimed. "Did you, Yigael?"

"Naturally," Dr Lem sighed. "So did Harriet, who has to dress the bruises afterwards. It's most disturbing."

"So are you going across the board too?"

"I don't think so. I'm old. And—and I wouldn't want to feel Chart had driven me off the planet where I've spent more than thirty years."

In another few minutes they dispersed to their respective homes, having agreed gloomily that now there was absolutely no other course open except to file a direct request on Earth for intervention by the government. And they had already learned, via the informat, that there was at most a one in ten chance of any action. Earth was remote, uninterested, incapable of ruling any of its daughter worlds, content to remain on speaking terms with them.

"If worst comes to worst," Jack said as they parted, "we shall have to send a delegate physically to Earth, to lobby the High Senate. That might help."

It might . . . But, as he greeted the anxious Pompy, Dr Lem could not convince himself that it would.

He wandered on to his verandah, as his custom was, and stared around. There was a faint haze over the goboard; it was active again. No doubt from now on there would be hordes of people heading for Yan, hoping to see this unprecedented event, this performance by Chart for an alien species—

Behind him, a call on the communet. He picked the floating extension out of the air and found Ducci looking at him.

"Yigael, Marc Simon came home."

"How do you know?" Last heard of, he had vanished

into Chart's ship, gone as completely as if he had been digested.

"I planted a remote alarm there, keyed to him. When I came in just now I found it signalling. He's not alone, either. The other person's female, but not Yannish. It definitely can't be Shyalee."

"Morag Feng?" Dr Lem tensed.

"I think that's the likeliest. But I can't pick up enough detail to be certain."

"He's not plugged into the communet there, is he? Can I call him over this remote of yours?"

"I'm afraid not. I could dispatch an extension if you like, but—"

"No," Dr Lem said with sudden decision. "I'll go call on him. If anyone might make Chart see reason, it would be one of those two."

"You don't have much chance of persuading Morag Feng!"

"I guess not." Dr Lem tried not to sound as hopeless as he felt. "But perhaps Marc."

XVI

"SHYALEE?" MARC CALLED. The house was in darkness—but of course on Yan it was never completely dark. There was always the shimmer of the Ring, even on a cloudy night.

He closed the street door behind him and advanced into the atrium. On his favourite stone seat overlooking the pool, a slim dark silhouette.

"Shyalee!" he cried.

"I'm sorry. No." The figure rose slowly. "It's Alice Ming."

"What are you doing here?" He strode towards her. "And where *is* Shyalee?"

"I don't know. But she won't be back here, I'm certain." Now Alice was in plain sight, her face grey in the silver radiance from the sky.

"I don't understand!" Marc burst out.

"Harry quit me." Alice's voice sounded as though she had wept for a long time, until there were no tears left. "And Shyalee has quit you. I was told so. By Harry. Oh—I'm wrong. That was force of habit, of course, calling him Harry. He's told me he is now Rayvor again, and will remain Rayvor permanently."

The fountain plashed under the words, like the muttering of an idiot who has stumbled across a sound that especially pleases him and will not stop repeating it.

"But why?"

"Because of what they believe Chart is going to do, of course! They believe that he's going to call back the dramaturges, re-create the golden age of Yan! They believe it's going to be real, and they'll have something real to be proud of!"

"Then they're crazy," Marc said slowly. "It will be what Chart's work always is, an elaborate drama. And when the performance ends—"

"Not here," Alice said. "Not on Yan. That's the way it is among humans. But Harry—I mean Rayvor explained it to me. Carefully. Speaker Kaydad had called him in, and Shyalee, and told them just what the difference is."

A huge growing coldness was forming in Marc's belly. He said, "And . . . ?"

"I didn't understand." Alice put her hand to her head and swayed a little. "He did tell me. He told me in Yannish, though. He said he never wanted to speak our language again. But the one thing he did say, over and over, was this: he said Chart would not be human when he finished. He said the greatest human artist was going to become an imitator of the Yanfolk. An ape, the other way around."

"Who else have you told, Alice?" Marc said at last.

"No one. I thought perhaps you would be the—the likeliest to understand." She checked, and gave him a curious stare. "Where have you been?"

"On a grand tour of the ancient relics with Chart and his mistress."

"Is she—is she really the same Morag Feng who was here so long ago . . . ?"

"Apparently." Marc had been so preoccupied, he had almost forgotten what he knew of that stale scandal.

"And is she determined to revenge herself for what I did?"

"I don't know." His tone was curter than he had intended.

"You're right," Alice said, passing her hand through her hair. "I shouldn't concern myself for something that can't any longer be helped. The best we can hope for now is to pick up a few of the pieces afterwards . . . Why did you come home? Just before you arrived, I was telling myself it was stupid to sit here in the dark expecting you, because you'd have heard about Shyalee and you'd have gone to the enclave again."

"I came back because Chart intends to take wilders and remove their brains, and programme them artificially to act out the rôle of dramaturges in his play."

"But—but that would be horrible!" Alice cried. "They're savages, but they're—they're living creatures! They're not dummies!"

"They will be when Chart gets at them," Marc said. "I was so revolted I told him to bring me home. I won't have anything more to do with the man." He shuddered. "And you know the worst thing? He literally didn't seem to understand my objection! All the way from the wilder continent he kept demanding, over and over, what I was so annoyed about!"

He pulled himself together by main force. "Well, I guess there's one obvious person we can go and talk to, and that's Dr Lem. Come on."

He put his arm around her and led her, quivering, out of the house.

"Aren't you Dr Lem?"

The voice was unfamiliar. For an instant he thought the chubby brown man who had hailed him was freshly off the go-board; then he realised it was this Erik Svitra, who had in fact arrived the other day and been adopted—according to rumour, without noticeable enjoyment—by Warden Chevsky.

"Yes?" Dr Lem said, pausing as he was about to turn a corner.

Erik came scurrying up to him. "Sorry to bother you, doc, but as a matter of fact I was on my way to see you." He swallowed hard. "I want to . . . Well, I want to apologise to someone. And I can't think of anyone except you. I mean, I had just enough credit to get me off this planet, just enough for a short go-board, and I'm getting out, but when I was on my way to the board I thought hell, a lot of this is my fault . . . Have you seen what it's like on the board right now? It's just flashing and flashing. People are pouring in!"

Dr Lem stared at him in the light of the nearby gloglobes. "Why are you leaving?" he demanded.

"Well, mainly I tipped off that news-machine, didn't I? So lots of people are going to come here, wanting to have their heads blown apart by this performance of Chart's and—hell, doc! The whole idea simply scares me silly! I can't explain. But I just thought, before I leave, I ought to tell someone I'm sorry, I didn't realise what I was doing."

He wrung his hands miserably. "Well, that's all, I guess—"

"There he is!" A call from down the street. They both turned. Hurrying towards them were Marc and Alice, holding hands.

"Why, I was coming to call on you," Dr Lem said gratefully. "Is that . . . ?" Peering through the multicoloured twilight, he checked. "Oh, it's Alice. Hello. Marc, I was coming to ask you—"

"Chart's going to do a terrible thing," Alice interrupted. "He's going to kidnap wilders and pith them, turn them into puppets for him."

Erik put his hand to his mouth. "These wilders—they're like the cousins of the natives here in Prell? I saw about them on the 'net; they got lots of recordings. But they're intelligent, aren't they? Got a language of a kind, got tools and things!"

He rounded on Dr Lem. "Say! They got laws against that, haven't they?"

"As a matter of fact they have," Dr Lem said. A great weight seemed to have dropped from him. "And oddly enough it was partly Chart's doing that they were passed. Explorers from Hyrax, sent out by the Quains, had caused such a scandal by capturing and exhibiting non-human intelligent life-forms that when they'd been deposed the successor government found no opposition at all when they tried to put such crimes into the galactic common-statute list. It's an offence on any inhabited planet to do what you just described. Here! Come on up to my place and let's consult the communet."

He swung around and set off the way he had come, his steps suddenly much brisker.

"And, come to think of it," he added when he had gone a few metres, "if you're leaving here anyhow, I wonder if you'd be willing to go—wherever you're going—by way of Earth."

Erik gaped at him. He said, "Clear to Earth from Yan? But that's almost the longest trip you can make across the go-board! Where'd I get the credit for a programme like that?"

"It could be arranged. In principle, though?"

"Hell, I've wanted to visit Earth ever since I was a kid! Mostly I have to go where I'm sent, though, by the drug-merchants I mainly work for."

"Then you have no need to worry about costs. I can programme you; it's a matter of elementary hypnotic indoctrination." Dr Lem hesitated. "There would be a condition, of course."

"I might have guessed. Hurt me with it."

"That you make it your first business, on arrival, to contact the committee on human-alien relations of the High Planetary Senate and report in detail on Chart's plans."

"That's all?" Erik said incredulously. "Why, sure! And cheap at the price!"

"Good." Dr Lem strode up the steps to the door of his house and pushed open the door. Pompy came crooning to meet him. Since he had been bound for the Yannish section of Prell he had left her at home.

Lights sprang up. Automatics whirred faintly, sensing the number of visitors and activating the services. "If you want refreshment, help yourselves," Dr Lem said, and headed straight for the communet console. Almost as he sat down his busy hands were engaged on its board.

"You know," Erik said, watching curiously over his shoulder, "that was the first thing that struck me about this here enclave of yours. You got communet facilities like I never saw any place else. Just for these—how many?—three hundred people and a few kids?"

"There's a purpose behind it," Dr Lem answered briefly. "You're quite right—these facilities are as advanced as what you find on Tubalcain, and in fact that's where the system was designed and built. The informat is so big, it could cope with a city of six or eight million people. Ah!"

On the screen, data flashed: "Galactic Common Statutes", and then a string of sub-heads. He punched the number of the one he wanted.

"Let him get on with it," Marc said, and Erik complied, turning away and coming to sit down on the big soft horseshoe-shaped settle in the centre of the room. Alice had leaned back and closed her eyes; there was an unhappy downward turn to the corners of her mouth.

"The communet has to be very comprehensive," Marc went on. "Matter of fact, it was partly because of the 'net that I moved out of reach of it, out of the enclave. Consider: here's this little community of humans, three hundred and some as you just commented, with no contact except via the go-board with any other human world—and you don't just make a go-board trip without preparation, on the spur of the moment. You have to be programmed with a hypnotic route-map, as it were. A long one may take hours and call for a very skilled practitioner to implant it firmly, especially if you're not a first-rate subject—"

"Don't tell me!" Erik said with a wince. "I used to be a fine subject. Then I ran into some stuff called *gif-mak*, and . . ." He mopped his plump brown face. "Never mind. What I mean, I get tired much more easily now. Still, if I have the chance to visit Earth for free, I'll risk it. Go on about the 'net you have here. Sounds kind of interesting."

"Well, it's to counteract the effects of isolation, you see. And, maybe more to the point, the pressure from this very stable, very strong Yannish culture next door. It got at me. In fact it's still there, right under my skin, so deep that half the time I find myself thinking sort of wistfully, 'I'd love to see the golden age of Yan brought to life! There's nothing I want more!' Which is true enough. I just don't want it so much that I can help Chart do this monstrous thing he was talking about."

"He actually wanted you to help him?"

"Oh, not literally wanted me to help catch the wilders—just to sort out the ambiguities and metaphors in the Mutine Epics which he's going to use as a script. Hey!" Marc sat bolt upright. "Dr Lem!"

"What is it?" Not looking around.

"Did you know that Shyalee left me, and Rayvor left Alice?"

"I hadn't heard. I can guess the reason, though. Have they been convinced that there's now a grand undertaking among their own people which they can join in?"

"More or less."

Dr Lem nodded and gave the board a final tap before turning his back on it. He looked very tired. He said, "I think it has adequate material. I've asked for a simulated verdict assuming that we send Erik here to

Earth and apply for an injunction to protect the wilders from Chart."

"Will it take long?" Marc asked.

"A minute or two, perhaps. By the way! Did I hear you say that Chart plans to use the Mutine Epics as the script for his performance? Can he? I'd always believed that even the *hrath* group among the Yanfolk didn't fully understand the text."

"Chart thinks he's found the twelfth book, the key which turns the Epics into a technical manual."

Dr Lem started. He rotated his chair again, and tapped on the communet board. "Where did he locate it? Did the Yanfolk give it to him?"

"He thinks it's compressed into the Mutine Flash."

Dr Lem stopped dead-still for an instant, then went on tapping. "Very ingenious," he said under his breath. "And it could so easily be true. So easily! If the dramaturges wanted to leave a guide for their descendants . . . Only the dust garbles the solar spectrum, correct?"

"That's what he thinks," Marc confirmed with genuine respect.

"Hmm! I wonder if it's even more than a set of instructions, then. I wonder if it could be a continual reinforcement, like our communet . . . You were asking about that just now, Erik. Marc was quite right to say it's a defence against pressure from our Yannish neighbours. Without it, there'd be a risk of people drifting away. For example, you've no doubt heard that sexual relations with a Yannish partner can be extraordinarily gratifying, and that fact alone would have been explosive even without the constant awareness of the relics, some of which we couldn't duplicate and none of which we understand."

"You mean," Erik said slowly, "this here enclave wasn't set up, like I assumed, to let the Yanfolk adjust to us humans, find out if they could stand living in our company. You make it sound exactly the opposite."

"Correct." Dr Lem gave a sad smile. "It's to find out whether we can put up with the Yanfolk."

"You're joking!" Erik said, wide-eyed. "What could these backward—?"

A voice from the communet interrupted him. "This is your informat speaking. Owing to data just coded into my banks by Dr Yigael Lem I have transmitted to Earth an orange emergency signal. Take no further action, repeat no further action, until instructed from Earth. The warden has been routinely informed of this alert."

Stunned silence. Erik was the first to break it. He said, "Well, then, I guess I don't get my trip to Earth after all."

XVII

TEN MINUTES LATER there was uproar. First to react, naturally, was Chevsky himself, who called up in such a state of fury that he could barely choke out coherent words. Marc, Alice and Erik sat nervously at Dr Lem's back while the old man patiently repeated, altogether five or six times, that this "orange alert" had been as much a surprise to him as to the warden.

"Instead of going on at me," he snapped finally, his patience exhausted, "why don't you ask the informat what it involves? I never heard of any such thing before!"

Chevsky, gulping great draughts of air, gave a vigorous nod. "I'll *do* that! And don't you try making any more trouble! We're sick of your self-righteous meddling, understand?"

The screen blanked. Almost in the same instant, there was a distant white flash through the window which gave a view of the Northern Range: the first of the summer storms was breaking out. The timing was so apt, one could almost have believed that the dramaturges were indeed returning to transform their planet into what the Mutine Epics claimed it once had been, a single centrally conceived work of art.

And then Ducci called, to say that the go-board had been remotely pre-empted by a trigger-signal from Earth, of which of course he as technical director had at once been notified, and to ask what in the galaxy was going on—and some of Dr Lem's neighbours, in hastily-donned gowns, came from bed to put the same question face to face—and in the end the old man had to throw up his hands helplessly and plead with them all to wait and find out.

But the next development was even more startling. From the spot where it had rested since its original landing, Chart's ship soared upward silently and began to drift in a north-westerly direction.

"He's not going away, is he?" Marc said, having run to the window which faced the ship. "I guess that would be too much to hope for!"

"No, that's a local course," Dr Lem said. "I'm an old man, Marc, and there were still many many starships when I was young. I've seen them on atmospheric courses before. He's just removing himself from our vicinity. Putting himself under the inarguable jurisdiction of the Yanfolk."

"What Harry told me—I mean what Rayvor told me," Alice said softly, "was that when he was finished here Chart would have become a copy of the Yanfolk. An ape in reverse."

"I think it's only too likely," Dr Lem said. "I was never so sure of the possibility that I made specific inquiries, but now I can see it's always been hanging over us—the risk that any social system strong enough to control millions of people for thousands of years might also be strong enough to take control of isolated humans."

"I don't get that," Erik said in a puzzled tone.

"Don't you?" Marc rounded on him, clenching his fists. "Hell, it's what could so easily have happened to me! Being caught up, being *digested*, into an alien pattern! There have been hints that this was happening, and I never realised until now. Dr Lem, there are so few children in the enclave, aren't there?"

"Right. And those few play at *shrimashey*, until one or more of them get crushed unconscious under the pile." Dr Lem wiped his face with the back of his hand. The night was not particularly warm, but they were all perspiring.

Suddenly, through the window facing the direction of the go-board, there was a brilliant blue glow which lit up the sky more brightly than the Ring. Erik jumped.

"What's that?"

"Unless I'm much mistaken, the arrival of the biggest consignment ever to use the Yan go-board," Dr Lem said. "A large party of humans, and a lot of equipment. Perhaps we ought to go and meet them on their way into Prell."

He was right in two respects. The party was enormous—more than a hundred people—and it was accompanied by a vast deal of equipment, most of which was autonomic and floated around under its own control like obstinate thistledown. He was wrong, though, about them heading for Prell. They made immediately towards the informat dome, and by the time Dr Lem and his companions arrived they found that Ducci, Chevsky, and several other people from the enclave were already present.

The dome, naturally, was not guarded. Anyone could enter it at any time. It was proofed by a coating of impervium against the risk of meteorites striking this far north of Kralgak, and its internal circuitry was all very solid-state indeed. Apart from its consultation consoles, its interior was featureless, a single hollow volume of a pleasant yellow material, normally visited only by an occasional maintenance worker except when it was used for town's meetings.

But now it was alive with strangers, who all seemed to know exactly what they were here for and were busy with mysterious little portable devices, touching the walls and floor, calling to one another in obscure technical jargon, discussing problems in little groups of three to six. Bewildered, Dr Lem stopped dead in the entrance and looked about him. He had forgotten to tell Pompy not to follow him, had only realised she had picked up his scent when he was already several hundred metres from home, and had decided against taking her back there. Now she lowered herself flush to the floor, all her legs tightly folded, and stared about her with the same astonished intensity as her master.

"This looks like," Marc began as he too took in the scene, and had to hesitate to be sure he was choosing the right image—"this looks like a military operation."

"I'm not quite sure what that means," Alice muttered. "Is it . . . ? Oh! You mean Yan is under attack?"

"I think it's more likely to be defended," Marc said. "Try and keep up with Dr Lem."

But Dr Lem wasn't going any further than the point he had just reached, for a tall woman in blue—dark-haired, dark-skinned, dark-eyed, with an authoritative manner, carrying a shoulder-mounted data-unit in a sleek blue case—had spotted him and forced her way through the unexpected crowd to confront him. She said, "You're Yigael Lem!"

"Ah . . . Yes, so I am."

"My name is Trita Garsonova." The data-unit was talking quietly, without interruption, to her right ear. "You filed information concerning a plan by Gregory Chart to pith and programme intelligent primitives."

"Was that what brought this—this army here?"

"Naturally. Did you learn of this plan personally?"

"No, I heard of it from Marc Simon over there—"

"There he is!" A bull roar among the crowd, and

Warden Chevsky came shouldering his way towards Dr Lem. "Just let me get my hands on that little—"

"Stop," said the woman in blue. She did something with a device hung from the belt of her tight coverall, and Chevsky stopped, his feet walking absurdly on the spot. He gaped at her.

"But I'm the warden here!" he burst out.

"You've just been indicted for gross dereliction of duty," the woman said. "You'll have a hearing. But any Earthsider temporarily on Yan is automatically under your jurisdiction, and as far as we can make out from the informat records there you not only haven't attempted to prevent Chart committing this disgusting crime, but you've actively encouraged him."

"I didn't know about—"

"Shut up," Garsonova said, and made another adjustment to her belt. Chevsky's mouth continued to move, but no sound reached them. Belatedly, Dr Lem recognised the effects of a police muffler. It had been almost forty years since he last encountered one.

There are advantages in living on Yan. Things like that can safely be forgotten.

"Good! Now . . . Ah yes: that's Marc Simon— and that's Alice Ming, according to my data—and that's . . . The brown man, the plump one?"

"A recent arrival. Erik Svitra."

"Oh, yes. A drug-tester. Did he come here to try and exploit *sheyashrim?*"

Dr Lem blinked, startled. "I'm not sure. I think perhaps yes. Uh—how do you know about the drug?"

Garsonova regarded him with cold eyes. She said, "Who in the galaxy do you think I am, doctor?"

"I—I've no idea. This is all so unprecedented!"

"And unprecedented things aren't part of the Yannish pattern," Garsonova nodded. "*I* see. No wonder you left it so long before you started putting pertinent data into your informat! I'm beginning to wonder why we bothered to set up such an elaborate device here; no one seems to have taken advantage of it! Still, you do appear to have a small hard core of people here with a trace of common sense. I want to assemble them somewhere convenient and have a talk. It's going to be like pulling hot coals out of a fire with our bare hands now, but we'll have to try."

And, less than thirty minutes later, in Dr Lem's house: the Shigarakus, Pedro Phillips, Hector Ducci, Harriet Pokorod, Marc, Alice and—more or less by accident—Erik Svitra. Garsonova glared at them.

"For your information, first of all, I'm the Chief Emergency Executive of the Standing Committee on Human-Alien Relations of the High Planetary Senate of Earth. Is that a resounding enough title for you, or do you want the rest of my official posts? I have eight altogether. I'm a qualified social psychologist, I'm a Degree Two Scholar in non-human linguistics, and I'm also a Scholar of Cybernetics and Data-processing. And right now I am very damned angry!"

They stared at her blankly.

She gave a sudden laugh, and leaned back in her chair. "Oh, not entirely with you, or your fellows in the enclave here. Mainly with the bureaucrats and politicians I'm responsible to. But I'm slightly angry with you, I have to admit. Didn't it cross any of your minds that letting Gregory Chart loose on a non-human planet was about the last thing Earth could possibly tolerate?"

"I think we all thought that Earth would be—would be unable to interfere," Dr Lem said after a pause. "In fact when we first asked our informat, that's what it replied."

"Hmm! Bad circuit-design there somewhere," Garsonova muttered. "Chart does his best to be a law unto himself; he's not, of course, but he tries hard. Obviously you tapped into the wrong category. Look, let me start by making clear what your situation is—if you don't already know."

"I think I do," Marc said. "Though I didn't realise clearly until this very night. This impression that Earth couldn't take a hand must be deliberate. It's to generate self-reliance and force self-confidence."

"Neatly put," Garsonova approved. "So far we've never run across a non-human star-travelling species. But we've encountered seven quasi-humanoid intelligent races, and one of them—this one—is so remarkably like us, we can be sure beyond a doubt we shall very shortly be faced with a race that's an out-and-out rival. The likeliest human group to encounter them is a distant colony, more remote than any of the present ones. That little outpost has to be able to stand up for itself, to make the right decisions, to behave with the right courtesy, firmness, whatever, to deal on level terms, as it were. You here on Yan are a—a test-bench. A pilot project. Didn't you realise?"

"After such a long time," Dr Lem said, "the awareness of that must have drifted to the backs of our minds."

"Hmm! Yes! Moreover several mistakes have been made, not here, but in the original planning. Still, we have a chance to correct them now. More to the immediate point: have any of you bothered to question your informat concerning the nature of the Yanfolk recently?"

They all looked blank. "I don't think I quite follow," Hector Ducci said at length.

"Galaxies in collision!" Garsonova exclaimed, putting her hand to her forehead in a pantomime of horror. "Why do you think we equipped this enclave with that informat, enough to service a full-sized city? I found the key data just by going to my own informat at home on Earth and tapping for it! It's been sitting in store for over ten years: *shrimashey*, the dramaturge principle, everything! And did none of you bother to . . . ?"

She let her hands fall to her sides. "No, that's absurd. Dr Lem, I must use your communet. Quickly!"

He made a vague gesture of invitation. She shot her hand into the air and whistled for a floating extension; the instant it reached her, she began to tap, then to talk.

"Category Yanfolk. Sub-category cultural manifestations. Sub-sub, *shrimashey* . . . I don't believe it. A blank screen."

"I've tried over and over, of course," Dr Lem said. "The most one ever gets is a rehearsal of various recordings. Tapes that sometimes go clear back to the original landing."

Garsonova's dark face seemed to have turned grey. She tapped a different code and spoke in condensed technical jargon to someone they didn't recognise, one of the team at work in the informat dome. They waited, horribly aware that something might have gone irremediably wrong, and tortured by the knowledge that they had no least conception what it might be.

"Got it," the man from the screen said. It had taken about three minutes. "Blocks on circuits QA-527 through QC-129. We'll clear them, but it'll have to be by hand. Slow job. Local only, luckily."

"You followed that?" Garsonova said, pushing the 'net extension aside with a trembling hand.

"Blocks on the data circuits!" Ducci burst out. "But I personally maintain those circuits!"

"Maintain, yes. But question the data they're putting out? Never!" Garsonova thrust back a lock of smooth dark hair from her face. "No wonder you let yourselves get tangled up in this! And to think we never spotted it until . . . Oh, never mind! I'll tell you! We *know* what *shrimashey* is, this fantastic population-control mechanism which looks like a drug-induced sadistic orgy. We know what the Mutine Flash is, and why it affects people the way it does—"

She checked, listening to the data-unit on her shoulder, which was still providing its automatic running commentary. Paling, she stared at Marc.

"You experienced the Mutine Flash from inside the Mandala?"

"Ah—yes, I did."

"Just before you commenced your translation of the Mutine Epics?"

"Y-yes!" Marc's voice shook, and his fists were so tightly clenched his nails were biting into his palms.

"Has anyone else done the same?"

"Morag Feng. Chart's mistress. Who persuaded him to come to Yan and perform."

"But this is terrible!" Garsonova said. "I— Yes, Dr Lem? Have you suddenly caught on to what's been happening?"

"I'm dreadfully afraid I have," the old man said in a gravelly voice. "You're trying to tell us that the Mutine Flash took control of Morag Feng, ordered her to go and find Chart—or more exactly, to find someone who could carry out the project of re-creating the Mutine Age. And Marc here, similarly, was instructed to make his translation of the Epics so that Chart would find his—his script ready and waiting."

"That's right," Garsonova said. "And what you've so cleverly been prevented from discovering, even though it was already informat data, is this. The Yanfolk, under the *sheyashrim* drug, are components of a superhuman organism whose collective brain consists in their lower spinal ganglia, the dramaturge—singular, not plural—which designed the wats and mandalas, and smashed the moon."

XVIII

FROM THE DAYS when he had first become interested in
the concept of the human enclave on Yan, and had
studied up the readily-available description of it which
the local informats on any planet carried as standard,
Marc recalled seeing that among the things it did not
boast were competitive commerce, public transport, and
representative government. Why bother, when there
were only a few hundred people, capable of being
linked over the communet or even, when a town's meeting was called at the customary quarter-year intervals,
assembled in a single spot?

But this town's meeting, called by Chevsky before he
was indicted and dismissed by his superiors from far-
away Earth, was unique.

Virtually the entire population of the enclave had arrived well ahead of time in the informat dome. It doubled as a public assembly hall when Hector Ducci hit
the right switch and created a horseshoe of seating from
its yellow floor. By the time Marc entered, it was almost full.

He had remained in his old home, not wanting to
return to the enclave. The air in Prell proper might be

full of the never-ending stink of *sheyashrim*. In the enclave, it was full of the odour of hatred. Chevsky had so
successfully convinced everyone that having Chart perform here would make them rich and famous, there was
now an almost universal dislike for himself, for Dr
Lem, for everyone who was suspected of having
thwarted the project.

Customarily the warden took the one seat facing the
audience. Tonight, when everyone was settled, Garsonova took it instead. Marc had had the idea of punch-
ing her name into the communet's encyclopedia facility,
and had been astonished to discover that she, like
Chart, rated a full article during her own lifetime—and
she was barely half Chart's age. Before entering government service, it appeared that she had been one of the
human race's leading experts on non-human intelligence, having pioneered important communication
breakthroughs with the Altaireans and the Denebolans.

"Why didn't they send someone like that to Yan?" he
had said despairingly to Dr. Lem.

"Because it's a big galaxy, and there aren't enough
people like that to go around."

The sullen hostility in the yellow hall could almost be
felt, like a chill fog. Most of it formed an aura around a
group near the front, centred on the Dellian Smiths and
others of Chevsky's former cronies. A corresponding
group had formed on the opposite side of the hall, directly in front of the platform where Garsonova was sitting in place of the warden, including Dr Lem's associates. Alice had attached herself to the fringes of this
latter group, having hung around at Marc's side ever
since Rayvor abandoned her. He liked her no better
than he had ever done, but he felt a pang or two of
sympathy.

He missed Shyalee. He missed her terribly. For all
her faults, he had found much happiness in her company. But the last time they had chanced across one
another, she had not even smiled at him.

Not one of the intruders from Earth, Garsonova excepted, had put in an appearance. They had done what they had come to do—check out and repair the informat which someone had tampered with—and faded away. But Erik Svitra was still here, and present; he was entitled, as were all humans whether passing through or resident.

"Extraordinary town's meeting," Garsonova said abruptly, and silence fell. "Called by the former warden, Guillaume Chevsky, to vote a motion concerning the enclave's support for or rejection of a proposed performance here by Gregory Chart."

"Chart said himself he wasn't here to perform for us!" called Dellian Smith loudly. "What's the point of this pantomime tonight?"

"If the people here so wish, they can apply for free go-board programmes to get them away from Yan until the performance is over—or permanently," Garsonova said.

"Miss a performance by Chart? When people travel scores of parsecs to try and be around when he's working?" That, Marc realised with dismay, was Hector's wife, Mama Ducci, still unconvinced after long argument.

"You miss the point. This is not a commonplace event, and the purpose of this debate is to acquaint you with data you may not so far have. First off, from the chair, I will read you an injunction which has been issued against Gregory Chart, to interdict him from a plan expressed verbally to Marc Simon—"

"That traitor!" Dellian Smith shouted. "We all know he wants to keep Yannish culture to himself, to be the only person in the galaxy who's recognised as an authority on it!"

"Who cares about the wilders, anyway?" From Boris Dooley, not one of Chevsky's closer associates but apparently—according to what Marc had heard—so incensed by Chevsky's dismissal that he had come down squarely on the wrong side. "The Yanfolk don't!"

"Perfectly true. They don't."

The words were slipped in with the precision of a scalpel. The voice, unmistakably, was Gregory Chart's. Garsonova whipped around in her seat. The sound had come from behind her, on the platform, and now, as though from an obscuring haze, two hitherto unseen human figures were taking shape: Chart himself, and Morag Feng, in unison dialling the anti-see units they wore at their belts.

"Forgive this subterfuge," Chart murmured. "But to have come here openly might have caused a distraction, and since we are legally entitled to attend we thought it best to exercise our rights."

"Rights?" Ducci was on his feet, shouting hoarsely. "You don't have any right to—"

"Yes, we do!" Morag snapped. "Any Earthsider transient or resident may come to one of these meetings!"

"And speak and vote," Chart glossed. "His vote, however, is progressively discounted once he has notified the informat of his intention to leave Yan again. I have no present intention of leaving Yan, and nor has Morag."

Garsonova said into a babble of noise, "You are quite correct. And your presence is fortunate. I now have the chance to serve you personally with the injunction which has already been imposed on the automatics of your ship for your attention. It prohibits you from taking away any of the Yanfolk known as 'wilders' from their customary living-zone, and specifically it forbids you to remove their brains or otherwise programme them for incorporation in—"

"I've already seen the injunction," Chart broke in. "I came here to say that while you may have caused me a lot of extra trouble by doing this, you haven't sabotaged the project as you hoped to. I'm going ahead. Not with your permission—I don't need it. But by direct invitation of the dominant species, the Yanfolk, in the person of their Speaker and the other *hrath*."

"Great! Great!" Dellian Smith shouted, and there was a ragged burst of applause. It was led by someone Marc didn't know. There were eight or ten strangers in the hall, who had come off the go-board as a result of the news-machine's tip-off. And they were only the first, he feared. More would follow.

Abruptly he jumped to his feet. "You told me you had no facilities for making Yannish androids! You said it would be too expensive and too time-consuming—"

"Oh, yes," Chart said. "It was you, no doubt, who put me to the extra trouble, or tried to. But the Yanfolk have solved the problem. They are presenting volunteers."

"What?"

"Volunteers. Take my word for it, they're genuinely willing. Indeed, they're excited about the prospect." Chart's deep eyes fixed Marc like spears. "Here are some more new data for you to compute with. I was right about the Mutine Flash; it is the key to the eleven other books of the Epics. My computer, built on Tubal-cain as you know, to the highest standards ever, has already worked out a tentative reading of its signal and every noon it's reinforced and clarified. As of now, for the first time in almost ten thousand years, the knowledge of the Yannish dramaturges is being recovered—and it's going to be applied. Convinced of this, numerous Yanfolk have offered themselves as vehicles for its expression, and among them you may be interested to know is a former friend of yours called Shyalee. So too is a male named Rayvor."

"You're going to pith them and—? Oh, no!" Alice was on her feet, poised to hurl herself bodily at Chart. Marc caught her arm.

"Save your breath," Chart said curtly. "There's no

law against accepting a volunteer to take *sheyashrim*. Right there beside you is a drug-tester, who's made his living for years by finding new ways of turning off people's reasoning faculties in favour of their autonomic reflexes. True?"

"And whether they are volunteers in your sense, or not, isn't up to you to determine," Morag said with a hint of smugness. "That's in Yannish jurisdiction, not human."

"I'm afraid it is," Garsonova said after listening for a moment to the data-unit on her shoulder.

"So there we are!" Chart said with a grin. "On the threshold of a newly glorious Mutine Age. Don't be too hard on Marc Simon, by the way. He was instrumental in helping me to develop this project. And in case you're worried about one final point, I don't propose to cast a vote in this matter. For one thing I'm an interested party; for another your opinions won't make a smidgin of difference. Morag, shall we leave them to it?"

"Just a second!" A reedy, forced voice. Dr Lem was rising. "Before you go, I have a further question or two." He patted his seat-neighbour, Marc, reassuringly on the arm. The poet had doubled over, head in hands, as the impact of what Chart had said about Shyalee reached him.

"Yes?"

"You have yourself viewed your—your *decoded* version of the Mutine Flash?"

"Of course. How else could I be so confident of eventual success, me a human dealing in Yannish concepts?"

"Did you know that after she had experienced the Flash your companion Morag—during her period of apparent insanity—put blocks on certain data-banks in this very informat?"

Morag paled and put her hand to her mouth. Chart rounded on her.

"What's all this nonsense?"

"I—I don't know what he's talking about," Morag muttered. But she was apparently giddy all of a sudden; she swayed visibly.

"And did you know," Dr Lem pursued, to the accompaniment of vigorous nods from Garsonova, Ducci and several others, "that there are similar blocks on some of your data-stores?"

"Rubbish!" Chart cried. "My computer is from Tubalcain, one of the most advanced ever built!"

"I can prove it," Dr Lem said, letting his thin old hands fall to his sides. "Just now you spoke of the *dramaturges* of Yan, plural."

"So?" Chart rapped. "Come to the point! Of course there were dramaturges plural!"

"It appears not," Dr Lem countered dryly. "I must admit I found it hard to credit, too, when Officer Garsonova told me, but I'm now satisfied of the truth. You see, these blocks planted in the informat had a purpose: to conceal from anyone making chance inquiries right here in the enclave the fact that when the Yanfolk enter *shrimashey*, they cease to function as individuals, and become part of a self-repairing collective organism. The process is much analogous to that of a cut healing, or a bruise: a certain prescribed number of cells replace a roughly similar number of damaged predecessors. This ought to have been widely known a long time ago, certainly some decades ago, because the mindless operation of the informat discovered it at least ten years back, and human intelligence is better at spotting patterns than any machine we've yet designed, even your vaunted ship's computer from Tubalcain.

"It was the—the cortex of that organism which was destroyed when the moon was shattered here. It was its higher nervous system. All that survived was its reflex functions. As individuals the Yanfolk have long been aware of this, and they have been looking for a substitute focus through which they could once more achieve what was once achieved by the dramaturge. Singular. The race in absolute rapport, every single member of it reduced to a component part of a planet-wide union. They have found not you, but *your ship*. And, thanks to Morag's interference while under the influence of the Mutine Flash, they have managed to hide the truth so completely that even you don't believe it."

"I . . ." Chart's mouth worked. "No!" he blasted. "No! Lies! Lies! Morag, come with me!"

He seized her anti-see unit, twisted it, and in the same moment dialled his own. They vanished even as Marc leapt up on the platform to try and stop them, and when the confusion simmered down, they were gone.

"Was—was that all true?" Dellian Smith said at last.

"As far as we can tell, yes," Garsonova said. "It was why we called you together, to inform you of it."

"Then you've got to do something! We can't let him recreate this monster!"

Beside him his wife Rachel mopped sweat from her face. She wasn't the only one.

"What would you have us do?" Garsonova said stonily.

"Well—blast Chart's ship from the sky if you have to! But stop him!"

"A few moments ago you were all for letting him— ah—perform here," Garsonova said, and let the point sink home. "No, that is the one thing we can *not* do. We are forever going to meet things without precedent as we spread through the galaxy. We are trying to evolve a code of principles which will serve us regardless of what happens. We will not wipe out somebody simply because what he does is unpredictable."

"Well, then, I'm going to get off Yan!" Smith barked. "You had no business turning us loose on a world like this, with—with . . . !"

"Right! Right!" A chorus. Everywhere in the hall people were scrambling out of their chairs.

A few minutes, and there were only Marc, Alice, Dr Lem, Ducci and Garsonova. And, hovering uncertainly by the exit, Erik Svitra.

"You're not leaving?" Garsonova said. "You'll get help if you want to—free go-board routes, a grant to resettle you somewhere else."

"I can't," Dr Lem said. "Not after more than thirty years."

"And I can't," Marc muttered. "If the Mutine Age can't be prevented, I guess someone ought to be around to witness it."

"And you?" Garsonova looked at Erik.

"Me? I just wanted to say I'm sorry I screwed things up. Just walked in and pow! Knocked things down!"

"Don't blame yourself," Marc said, staring at the floor. "That's the history of man."

Erik bit his lip, hesitated a second longer, and went out.

XIX

"I AM REMINDED," Dr Lem said, "of somebody I haven't thought of in years: my grandmother."

Marc thought for a moment. Suddenly he nodded. "I know exactly what you mean," he agreed.

They were inside the informat dome. It had been equipped—almost casually—with vidscreens more numerous and more flexible than those Dr Lem had seen in Chart's ship. Under its impervium protection they could reasonably expect to survive whatever happened as a result of the re-creation of the Mutine Age.

Also, orbiting Yan, there were scores of remote spyeyes, and preparations had been made to record, analyse and study whatever unpredictable phenomena might now begin. There had been several already. Last night, following the departure of the last party across the goboard, the Yanfolk had destroyed the human enclave. They had walked out of their own part of Prell carrying torches, sledge-hammers and axes, and systematically reduced all trace of the alien buildings to smoking rubble.

Marc and Dr Lem had sat here and watched the process. The Yanfolk were obviously aware of the hov-

ering remotes which relayed the scene to the informat
dome, but they made no attempt to attack them.
Clearly, they wanted what happened to be made known
as widely as possible among mankind.

But there had been a strange savage joy in what they
did.

"You mean Earth," Marc said eventually.

"Yes. It's a strange feeling for an old man to have,
Marc!" Dr. Lem shifted his elderly bones on his padded chair, from which he had hardly stirred, except to
walk about the hall and stretch himself, since the go-
board was inactivated by a signal from space. There
were standby demolition charges ready, just in case the
totality of the Yannish organism proved able to re-start
its subtle power-fields, those space-straining contor-
tions which literally enabled a traveller to walk a parsec
with every pace.

"A good feeling for a young one," Marc said. And
they both knew exactly what they were referring to:
this sudden reassuring sensation that even across the
gulfs between the stars the mother planet was doing her
best to support and protect her offspring.

"Did you ever realise that we were—what did Officer Garsonova call us?"

"A pilot project?" Dr Lem said. "I guess I must
have, now and then. Something kept me here on Yan,
even though I often felt I was wasting my time and my
talents. Now I know I have an important use to put
them to. The automatics will take care of a great deal
of the raw information—but what better witnesses
could there be for this unprecedented event than a psychologist and a poet?"

"What's Chart doing at the moment?" Marc said
gruffly. He felt inadequate for the task which he had
accidentally taken on.

"I don't think you can talk about Chart doing anything any longer," Dr Lem said. He flicked a screen to
life, and they saw the Mutine Mandala shining in min-

iature, receiving from space the focused beams of the sun which was in fact drifting towards the western horizon. It had shone since before dawn; Chart's ship had launched a group of relay satellites which ensured that there would always be beams directed at the proper angle to excite the play of light and colour from the crystal pillars. Like a straggly pencilled line, a succession of Yanfolk were processing towards, and across, and out of, the mandala.

"Being programmed," Dr Lem said. "Those are what we mistook for the dramaturges: the ordinary Yanfolk, given a particular stimulus."

"Why did the dramaturge wait so long?" Marc muttered.

"I can guess," Dr Lem said with a sigh. "And the informat seems to agree with me, by the way. When its most ambitious plans are under way, ordinary nervous tissue won't cope, particularly if it's in competition, in an individual, with a higher nervous centre, a brain capable of thinking for itself. What happened to the Yanfolk was a colossal nervous breakdown, which resulted in the shattering of the moon. The reduced awareness of the collective organism was frightened. It's immortal, or effectively so—you realised that, of course?" With a glance at Marc.

"Yes."

"Therefore it was in no hurry to repeat the mistake it formerly made. It waited its chance to try again, hoping—oh—hoping that the Ring would ultimately dissipate, and that Kralgak would become passable again, and that the wilders would be re-integrated into the species . . . But what's the use of hypothesising about something which is as far ahead of us as we are of the amoeba?"

"I don't agree," Marc said after a pause. "I think intelligence is a continuum, and that any rational creature able to transcend determinism—reflex—can in some sense communicate with and understand any other. There may be a gulf of the same kind as there is between a poet and a mathematician; one may have mental processes the other can't imitate, because they're not intrinsic to him. But one can understand the goals of the other, and to some extent the end products."

"Perhaps," Dr Lem conceded. "Just as you or I could share the excitement of a cosmogonist whose equations have balanced, indicating that his theory about the origins of the universe are logical ones, without either being able to grasp the factors involved or apply the necessary operators to them."

"You take my point exactly," Marc said. "If we are to call any being intelligent, there must be at least one area we can share and communicate about. The rest—well, they may be as inaccessible as the core of a gas-giant."

"I wonder whether, one day, there might be a chain of such shared areas of experience, tenuous links that connect all the intelligent races in the galaxy, such that every thinking species has some data about each of the others, at tenth or fiftieth or thousandth hand."

"That may take a million years," Marc said.

"But it might be starting here and now," Dr Lem countered. "And—"

He broke off. The informat had flashed at them. "Chart's ship is taking off," it said. "Following an atmospheric course."

"If it is starting," Marc said, "I wonder if it will be anything we can understand."

"What's the good of guessing . . . ? I wish I had Pompy with me, you know. What a foolish thing to say here and now!"

"Where is she?"

"I sent her off-planet with the Duccis; she's always been fond of Giuseppe, and I thought it unfair to force her into this even if I had stupidly decided to play the hero."

"Is that how you think of this?" Marc demanded.

"No. To be candid, no." Dr Lem wiped his face; it was glistening with sweat. "It's not bravery which kept me here, but obstinacy. Once upon a time I had this ambition, to unravel the mystery of Yan. And now it's turned out the mystery hasn't been a mystery for years, and the solution's only been kept from me by an ingenious trick played on this informat"—a gesture around the yellow hall they sat in. "And I feel annoyed! I feel cheated! I feel I want to do something to compensate."

He hesitated. "And," he concluded, "I have learned to love this planet."

"A field has been detected," said the informat. "The rain of meteorites on Kralgak has reduced by forty per cent—by forty-four per cent—by forty-nine per cent—it is extrapolated that the meteorites will cease completely in one minute twenty-two seconds from the mark. Mark."

"After all your work with the Mutine Epics," Dr Lem said, "have you any clear idea what the dramaturge was trying to do?"

"Yes," Marc said. "Control the universe."

After which the sudden flood of startling images made conversation impossible.

Once more the form of a moon hung over Yan, but this time it darted back and forth like the racing hand of a weaver, or a potter, imposing design on crude shapeless materials. The night, over most of the planet's northern hemisphere, had been equable and mild, with a few clouds and only one summer storm, far around the world's shoulder over the ocean. Little by little the air grew charged, and lightning began to strike randomly. The aurorae swirled towards the equator, not in disciplined patterns as on the night of Chart's arrival, but in mere eddies, such as would attend the wake of a boat crossing choppy water at high speed.

And there were brief hiatuses in the glow from the Mutine Mandala as the full blast of the local sun in empty space was concentrated for a fraction of a second on Chart's ship, to power it in the tasks which now it was being called upon to perform.

The Gladen Menhirs, marching in their serried line around the world, had suffered under the bombardment of meteorites. The ship paused here and there where gaps occurred in the line, or where one of the vast stone columns had been chipped. The land nearby shifted. Rock rose of its own accord, flowed as it rose, formed tidily into a match for the rest of the menhirs, heated until it was molten and then chilled to ambient in less than the twinkling of an eye. As the process continued, the vast stone blocks began to quiver.

"Minor seismic phenomena," reported the informat.

As yet, though, there was nothing that could penetrate the impervium shell of the dome in which they watched, anchored to the planetary crust.

"How's it done?" Marc breathed, and didn't expect an answer, either from Dr Lem or from the informat. Analysing a technique like this would have to wait until much, much later. This was not part of human science, this means to make rock ring like a handbell.

Next, that curious hollow mountain-top which Marc had visited with Chart and Morag, with the seating for thousands facing a blank wall. The ship stooped over it, carved with a stabbing laser-beam a pathway up the slope of the peak, and Yanfolk who had been patiently waiting at its foot began to approach it.

"That's a key part of the dramaturge," Dr Lem said with absolute certainty. "That's a—a cortex for it. Thousands of individuals cut off by walls of rocks from the exterior universe."

It was obvious from their jerky gait that the Yanfolk were under the influence of the *sheyashrim* drug—but it was known that they had been brewing it in every city on Yan, not just in Prell, and the total quantity must amount to enough to dose every Yannish adult a hundred times over.

Next: the Mullom Wat . . . and the ship spun, insanely, a few metres above the water of the ocean, until it created a miniature cyclone and sucked up a huge column of whirling mist and spray. On top of the Wat itself a globe of water formed, remained intact against wind, against gravity. What the purpose of that was, they dared not even guess. But there was something in the globe of water. It gleamed now and then, apparently fixed although the water revolved.

And minor tasks: removal of a little pink thing, barely six metres high, from a post-glacial scree on the flank of Mount Frey; its installation on a nearby crest—assembly of uncountable fragments from beneath a landslide, into a shivering, howling framework of sour green light . . .

There seemed to be no end to the details of this preparation. Marc felt himself yawning as the screens relayed all these scenes to him, and was faintly surprised that he was still capable of feeling tired. When one could not make head or tail of what was being shown, though . . .

"And that's the power-source!" Dr Lem said suddenly.

"What?" Muzzily, Marc sat up and stared at the screens; to his amazement, he had indeed managed to doze off. He had a vague half-memory of the informat saying something, and tapped for a repetition.

"Major seismic events," he heard. "Crustal slippage on all continents."

What?

"Did you say power-source?" he said, turning to Dr Lem. The old man didn't remove his gaze from the screens. Now they showed vast storms, brilliant lightnings, mountains crumbling, the ocean boiling into colossal waves. Also, penetrating even the impervium dome, there was a grinding, screaming, rasping, mindbreaking drone.

"The informat is still analysing," Dr Lem said. "But I think that's what it must be. Informat?"

"Yes, Dr Lem?"

"Was it the intention of the dramaturge to convert the kinetic energy of the moon's rotation into propulsive power for the entire planet Yan?"

"Current data indicates this as a likely assumption," the machine said unemotionally. Marc caught his breath.

"In order to undertake a voyage throughout the galaxy?"

"The probability is high."

"You were right to say the dramaturge's ambition was on a universal scale," the old man said to Marc. And continued to address the informat.

"Is it now intended to make the planet's crust slip on its molten core, so that the resulting energy can be tapped and stored for the same purpose?"

"The probability is high," the machine repeated.

"But—!" Marc leapt from his chair. In his mind the picture was instantly vivid, more vivid than anything he had seen on the screen surrounding them. "But you can't do that, not without smashing the planet to bits! We'll be *killed!*"

"It's already happening," Dr Lem said glacially. "Look!" He pointed at the screen which showed what was happening along the coast of what had been the wilders' continent. The ocean was dissolving into steam and rocks were being tossed out of it like pumice from a volcano. Also there were real volcanoes on two—no, four—no, *five* of the other screens . . .

And the floor shifted under them, as though the impervium dome were a beached boat just touched by the rising tide.

XX

"MARC! MARC!"

He was aware, but distantly, as though through a grey mist, that Dr Lem was staring at him, talking to him, half-turned around in his chair. Also there were the artificial, remote, miniaturised images: the volcanoes, the tidal waves, the storms . . .

No matter. That was on the wrong level of awareness. That was single-pointed perception. That was petty. That was obsolete. There was something infinitely better.

With the last trace of normal, human-style consciousness, Marc Simon the poet recalled a question he had put to the informat when the technicians from Earth had removed the blocks concerning the Yanfolk which had so efficiently and for so many years deceived the inhabitants of the enclave. He had asked what kind of field, or force, united the separate members of the Yanfolk when they entered *shrimashey*, and how it could be detected. And the informat had stated that it could not be detected by any instrument thus far developed by human science; however, so many other fields, forces, space-continua, rings, sets, conditions and plena were already known that it must certainly lie within the limits set by *n* aleph* and the pi-to-the-e space of the go-board. Over six thousand seven hundred spaces were suspected which could occupy these parameters.

The likeliest detection instrument, the informat had declared, was a human nervous system.

Marc Simon was just discovering that it was right.

Skeleton . . .

Is a man aware that he has bones? Unless a gash opens the skin and muscle, shows the pinkish-white bone—say at the shin—there is only awareness of rigidity, articulation, and support.

Hot rock. Liquid but so compressed as to be rigid. Skeleton.

Muscles . . . Supple, on the basis of bone. It took anatomists years, decades, centuries of patient cutting up of corpses to discover how the muscles set in, what bones they anchored to, that there were muscles not subject to the will.

Metabolism . . .

They called it second wind, and it was in fact a subtle chemical reaction triggered by the inadequacy of breathing.

(All this very rapidly, and at the same time:)

Nervous system . . .

For millennia human beings did not know that they were thinking with their brains.

What was left of Marc Simon was laughing. It was the cruellest kind of laughter he had ever imagined: the dirty insulting laughter of a man who thinks it funny to stick out his foot and trip a cripple. But it wasn't Marc Simon who was laughing, as he had known Marc Simon. It was that which was left of Marc Simon when the dramaturge's neural currents took over his autonomic reflexes. There was intent behind that. There was the desire to make these upstart simians from Earth respect the being, the personality, of the Yan(folk).

What Dr Lem saw was his companion lying on the

floor, roaring with hysterical mirth. But he, not having been taken out of himself, also saw the images on the screens, and felt the dome shifting as the solid land under it became first plastic, then molten, then fluid. The informat reported unemotionally that the exterior temperature was eight hundred thirty degrees.

He thought of the watchful devices from Earth, orbiting overhead, and was a little less afraid of dying than he had been a minute ago.

The planet strained, cried out, struggled, moaned. Its crust cracked, its mountains collapsed, its ocean churned and now literally began to boil. Meanwhile, the Yanfolk in the grip of their drug concentrated, con cen tra ted c o n c e n t r a t e d

Like a man retaining command of his reason after finding himself without warning under water, seeing the glimmer of light at the surface, working out that he must swim to it while the cold in his nostrils presses and presses on the precious vanishing store of oxygen luck enclosed in his lungs.

And unable to stop himself wondering whether he will survive.

"You should not," Marc thought inside his head to the dramaturge, "have risked proving what you could do to me or any other human. You over-reached yourself once. By insisting on this audience you have made certain of over-reaching yourself again."

There was a quiet content deep within him. It had nothing to do with him, personally, the individual Marc Simon. It was racial. Collective. Like the rival, the dramaturge.

Meantime the planet strained and sweated and creaked.

"Do I understand because I came close to understanding Shyalee?"

That was a fraction of himself-as-was—barely enough to formulate the question.

But there was not enough of Shyalee in the dramaturge to know what he was talking/thinking about.

Awed, Dr Lem watched the spectacle on the screens. On the downlands of Hom the silver-tailed deer-like creatures fled from the heat which made the ghulnut-trees crackle into flame. The Plateau of Blaw cracked and trembled and cracked again, and the neat orchards, the tidy fields of Rhee scorched, convulsed, tossed their plants to the wind and let go of their ancient soil in the form of dust.

Meantime the image of the sun, on the day side, was perceptibly smaller.

Dr Lem nodded. Yes. What he had long loved was dying. And of its own free will.

He caught a glimpse, through a remote which had not previously been activated, of a tribe of wilders on a hillside, dancing exultantly as though their whole bodies had been caught up in a colossal shared orgasm. Two or three children stared at them dazedly, and one whimpered for food. But to the dramaturge that was irrelevant, as though a cell of skin had been damaged through the failure of a microscopic capillary.

The sun grew smaller yet in the sky, and darkness blotted out the blue.

He did not look at him, but was aware of him, lying on the yellow floor apparently unconscious.

So far, so good . . . except that there is simply not the energy for the dream to come true.

(That was recognisable as himself, colouring the—the concepts. Not words. Words were too small to communicate with this incredible mind.)

Like a man running with a gash in his femoral artery, losing so much blood at every step that no matter were he the galaxy's finest athlete he must fall before the finish.

The planet bled. Heat roared from cracks in the bed

of the Ocean of Scand. Mountains crashed into valleys. The great desert of Kralgak began to slide away from the geographical relationship it had maintained for ten millennia, as though its friction against the northern and southern continents had abruptly become less than its friction against the molten core below.

If I had enough contact with my body, I would weep. It makes me afraid, it makes me terrified, to see this happen!

The planet was far from its orbit now, curling outward towards the bleak deeps of space, and the Earth-sent monitors and remotes paced it faithfully. The merest quiver of its dying agony must be noted, studied, interpreted . . .

Marc wanted, unexpectedly, to scream. More than he wanted to weep. But that was a brief horror. It ended with the moment at which the Mutine Mandala ceased to shine. The roiling clouds of smoke and dust from the volcanoes had blotted out even the immensely magnified solar radiation which Chart's satellites had caught and concentrated for it.

It was like stepping from a hot to an icy planet on a single stride across the go-board. And there was a—a voice? Not quite. A personality. A presence. (All this was being remembered in the brain belonging to Marc Simon. It might never be fully understandable. It might be the raw material, one day, for a poem. It might be the making of a style which would enable tens of millions of people to say, "Ah, that's by Marc Simon!" But it was also as cruel as a hot branding iron, and the message he could read as though it were flayed into his skin told him that it would scar him for ever and ever and ever and ever and ever and ever . . .)

They built that Mandala as you build computers. You understand?

Yes.

I am using a person you called Gregory Chart. I

would have used the one you called Morag Feng. Only she was used before, and she is so tainted with the now-vanished message of the Mandala—

Yes.

This is the story of the Mutine Epics. It is a story without an ending. Only a conclusion. There will be nothing left, in a very little while, except a cold bare ball of rock shrouded in chill mist, and certain strange relics which performed certain actions.

Yes.

(It seemed to be seeking reassurance from him, every few moments, asking that he at least would remember and recount.)

Once there was a planet whose people called it Yan. It was fertile, hospitable, even beautiful. A species evolved on it which was so far beyond your little isolated individuality that you can have no conception . . .

Go on. You lost me.

No. I was reconsidering. You do have a conception. It is what frightens me.

Frightens?

Yes. You are a poet, as Gregory Chart is/was an artist (but not will be because he is burning out). There is a mode of communication among you which is like that among my/our species, but which cannot take control of you. I am dying because while your dreams lure you my/our dreams had the power to drive us.

I think I understand that.

Yes, you do. And because you understand it is right that your isolated, lonely, separated scraps of protoplasm should do what I/we failed to do.

If it had been possible, the planet would have begged for mercy. Its crust was skidding on its core, the primeval magma was bursting out like arterial blood, its last few surviving inhabitants were struggling to breathe. On its tormented surface a human-built impervium dome bobbed like a bubble on a rough river. The Smor had long ago been choked with debris and carrion. One after another the remotes were failing as landslides overwhelmed them, or crevasses opened and swallowed them up. Prell had gone to join its predecessors under water, but this water had been boiling, now was cooling or seething or . . .

The dream broke you.

Because the dreaming part of me/us has never had to fight the harsh intractable reality of matter and energy. Do you see?

Yes. For you, who were the sum of the lower ganglia of a multi-million species, the universe was a concept, to be toyed with. Survival was dealt with by your separate members. So was hard work. So was reproduction. In other words . . .

Think it. I am past being insulted. I am reduced to a series of resonances in the badly-adapted circuits of a human computer, and one point of contact with your species: the failing brain of a once-great artist, whom I infected with my own vision . . . and burned out, as I burned out the victims of my earlier grandiose ambition.

You no longer say/think I/we.

There is no more "we". What oxygen in the air of the planet Yan has not been consumed in this colossal burning will shortly fall on its rocks as snow. We are half a light-year from the sun it used to circle. Complete the thought you had in mind.

You're insane.

If sanity consists in doing what the universe permits, then—yes.

The last of the remotes failed. The informat said, "It is necessary now to convert to survival mode. Do not be alarmed. Adequate supplies and protective equipment are available to ensure your safety."

Dr Lem was shaking as though he had been an inch from death and not realised until the danger was past. His teeth chattered and his eyes were watering. He could barely make out Marc's body writhing on the floor. But none of the medical automatics had come to attend it.

It is something to have had a dream.

It is nothing to have become that dream. And not even a dream in myself. I am a fading echo in computer circuits, poorly adapted to resonate with my type of consciousness. Were it not for the minimal cerebral activity I can still detect in Gregory Chart, I would already have been—

Stop.

Marc sat up slowly, every limb aching as though he had been whipped and then crushed under very heavy weights. He heard Dr Lem say, "Marc—?"

And put his head in his hands, and wept, for Shyalee, for the dramaturges of Yan, for the Mutine Epics, for the dream that became the dreamer and when the time came to wake ceased to exist.

A voice said, "Malfunctions aboard the ship of Gregory Chart passed the permissible percentage. An automatic survival programme has been instituted. Requests for emergency assistance are being automatically broadcast."

"Marc?" Dr Lem said.

Marc looked at him and saw that he was whiter than paper. He said, "It was like what Chart did on Hyrax. There was a dream. It ended, and it had to be paid for. Only this time the dreamer was aware that it was dreaming. It was able to plan during the dream how to avoid payment."

"I don't understand," Dr Lem said, staring.

"Nor do I," Marc said. He felt his cheeks. They were wet. He looked at the little glistening drops he had transferred to his fingertips and found them very funny. He began to laugh. After a moment Dr Lem joined in, in a high old-man's neigh, with the hysteria of relief at having not after all been part of the dream which now was ended.

XXI

"YOU KNOW MARC better than I do—or the automatics. Is he all right?"

Softly, from Trita Garsonova, that extraordinary woman who had so unexpectedly brought the support and comfort of grandmother Earth across the parsecs when everyone on Yan imagined it to be out of reach.

Dr Lem cast a worried glance in Marc's direction. He seemed to be sitting there quite calmly . . . but of course he had undergone terrible strains during the death of the planet Yan—torn apart by its own internal fires, then frozen in the wastes of interstellar space, as a result of the release of forces which humans admitted they could not control. And of those who had been most directly exposed to such forces, at least two were unlikely to recover. Both Gregory Chart and Morag Feng were completely insane.

"We're worried," Garsonova whispered. "He had such an emotional commitment to the Yanfolk."

"Like Chart?"

"Oh, on the contrary! Chart's commitment was only to himself; it was his ambition to be admired by us, by mankind, when he had transcended our natural limitations and conquered the mental territory of another race. When he found he couldn't . . . But Marc is different."

"Yes," Dr Lem said. "Marc is different."

And at about the same instant, Marc thought, "Ah, of course—I'm on *Earth* . . . ?"

It seemed that he had a moment ago re-connected with his physical personality, after a period of non-time, after mere interval. He tried not to show alarm as he groped for memory. A go-board trip? Logically, yes. Since he was on Earth.

And not just on Earth. In a committee-hall of the High Planetary Senate. He was distantly aware of that fact, as though he had been told it by someone he didn't know well and didn't particularly trust. He stared in vague surprise at the high-roofed hall, at the people present—of all skin-colours, wearing an amazing range of garb, each seated at an informat-desk which tapped such stores of data that it was rather like combining them all into a collective . . . organism?

"Hello, Marc," a voice said without sound. Deep in his brain, on a level he was not consciously in control of.

But there was a familiar accent to the message. It reminded him of a slender, graceful body pressed to his own, uttered kinesthetic and tactile signals and a scent like nightbreeze drifting off the orchards of Rhee.

He felt himself, in Earthside clothing, his Earthly weight pressing him into a padded chair, one of a whole line of people facing these committee-members under an illuminated ceiling designed to duplicate Earthly sunlight. It was comforting to be so thoroughly reinforced by all the ancient racially-familiar symbols. So comforting, indeed, that he was able to answer.

"Hello."

"You know what I am. If you want me to be more precisely Shyalee, for example . . . ?"

But she was a few bones, charred, then frozen. He made a negative.

"She was never you. Even at the end, her consciousness drowned out with *sheyashrim,* she wasn't you."

"Define me, then."

"What little of the dream of Yan survived the extinction of the species that created you, and then the intolerable pressure of a starship computer which rejected you—and which now must endure the reflex prejudices of another race."

The . . . Could one use the term? Yes, it was inescapable? The dramaturge said, "Also Chart. He was arrogant, and tried to fight me. He had intended to use the Yanfolk as a stepping-stone to an ambition of his own. You are humble. You are the greater artist."

"Nonsense!" Marc snapped—silently. "Merely a younger man. Does age mean nothing to you at all?"

There was a pause. During it, Marc noted that someone who had helped co-ordinate data concerning the fate of Yan was delivering a prepared speech. He ignored the flow of words. He had something in his memory which transcended them.

"Yes," the presence inside his head indicated abruptly. "The proportions are different, though . . . You do understand what Chart originally overlooked, the most obvious explanation for the thousand-year quiescence of the Yanfolk?"

"I've talked about this with Dr Lem. He sensed it from the moment he arrived there. Exhaustion." And, hastily, he added, "What I and so many others mistook for fulfilment."

"In a way it was . . . but exhaustion is closer. Superorganism or not, I/we was/were worn out. It is not to be regretted that I/we died."

"?"

"Of course. What survives is only your awareness of what I/we were. I found something relevant in your mind; here!" And, as though a tape were being replayed: the memory of talking to Dr Lem, speculating about the chain of comprehension which might ultimately link all the intelligent species in the universe. It shone briefly in his mind like a necklace, every jewel of which was more brilliant than the Mutine Flash. He almost cried out for the shock.

At once melancholy darkened the vision, and he realised why. There were certain species doomed never to know whether the vision had a chance of coming true.

"I will now call on Marc Simon for his subjective analysis of . . ."

"I sense you appreciate why the planet had to die. But can you make them understand too?"

"That's not up to me. That's up to you."

He was already rising to his feet, staring out over the serious, intent faces before him. All strangers. But all the personification of that comforting grandmother, Earth: isolated, perhaps stupid, certainly insensitive and beyond doubt inquisitive simians, worried by having lately heard about a creature, or a being, which regarded the displacement of heavenly bodies from their orbits as no more than a supreme effort of will, like a man lifting a heavy rock.

And it was up to him to make them see not only what was wrong with that approach to the universe, but also what had—after a fashion—been right about it . . .

He began to speak.

It was his voice that was heard in the hall, but it was not his mind that shaped the message. He listened, along with everyone else—though only he perceived the movements of tongue and lips, sensed the strangeness of having to draw breath. (Shyalee who had not needed to interrupt her kisses) . . .

"The real problem was this," he heard himself say. "There was only one intelligence on Yan. And a single consciousness is simply not various enough to cope with the universe."

There were nods around the hall. The data-

processing devices which mankind had adopted as
prosthetics to underpin its own fallible reasoning power
had presumably already pointed out something of the
kind, just as the informat on Yan had known about
shrimashey and would have told anyone and everyone
about it had not the relevant data-circuits been cun-
ningly blocked.

"By ten thousand years ago this intelligence, confined to its own resources, had exhausted the possibili-
ties of its own planet and wanted to explore the local
galaxy. It had treated Yan exactly as a human might
treat his home: in other words, made it over to conform
with a set of ideal preferences. It had devised the tele-
scope, but the techniques which led us to the starship
and the go-board were down an avenue of knowledge it
had not discovered. To transport itself to the stars it
would imagine no other vehicle than its home planet,
and to launch the planet it could conceive no other
means than conversion of the kinetic energy of its moon
into propulsive force.

"To help the individuals of its species survive the
projected voyage, it fined down their characteristics,
sacrificed their imagination and initiative in favour of a
totally stable, perfectly self-regulating reflex process,
ideal just so long as the goals of the race were so far
ahead of those of the individual that the latter were
negligible.

"Only the moon broke apart.

"The kinetic energy which should have catapulted
the planet out of its solar system paid no greater divi-
dend than earthquakes, tidal waves and the formation
of the Ring.

"If there's a human experience which corresponds to
the shock of that event, it can only be amnesia. The—
the Yan, one has to say, considering it was a world-
wide awareness—the Yan, then, became . . . unconscious. Its components systematised what they recalled
into obscure poems, but they could no longer even in-

terpret the data compressed into the Mutine Flash, which was what might be called a set of notes, prepared in just the same way a human might write down references, or programme a computer, before tackling a particularly complex and demanding task, to inform him at every stage not merely what had to be done next but what had been done up until now.

"Only the pattern in the Mutine Flash was as much a conscious process as the web of neural currents in the brain. It grew frustrated, and of its own accord began to search for ways to complete its assignment. It found me, when I ran the crazy risk of witnessing the Flash from inside the Mandala; similarly, it found Morag Feng, and through her Gregory Chart.

"By the time the Yan consciousness was functioning fully again, though, humans had been on the planet for a long while. And humans, and the human artefacts it investigated, such as the computer from Tubalcain built into Chart's ship, were calculating with concepts far beyond its grasp. It could never, for instance, have imagined the go-board—not because it was incapable of understanding the physical principle, but because it could not envisage the distribution of its parts among the planets of scores of different suns.

"Yet it could not bear to believe that these sons of monkeys were intrinsically its superiors. It wanted to make some colossal gesture to impress them. Unfortunately there was only one such gesture in its repertoire, and it failed. You might compare it to what Chart did on Hyrax. A dream was brought to life, but it had to end with an awakening in the real world. The real world rejected it. Natural law would not permit the hurling of the planet Yan through null-space to another sun. The planet broke!

"Why did not the Yan foresee this? Perhaps it did. If it did not, then the reason must lie here. The Yan was never a scientist. It was an artist. In the terms we invented to accommodate the symbology of the Mutine

Epics, it was a dramaturge, whose highest ambition was to convert the universe into a work of art. But if it can be one, then it is one already, and all we can be is the audience for it.

"Regardless of whether the Yan knew all along that its plan was doomed, we can be sure that it realised the truth when the end drew near. And it did something which I'm terribly glad I shall never have to do. We're lucky, we humans. We don't bear, each of us, a total responsibility in our dying. We can accept the knowledge that we exist *sub specie aeternitatis*—against the perspective of all time and all space—because there are more of us to carry on.

"The Yan, though, had to decide, under the shadow of its terrible failures, whether or not it wanted to be remembered, and how to ensure that it would be. Think! That had to be settled once for all, in the counterpart of the twinkling of an eye."

A chill seemed to pass through the hall, as though Time himself had brushed them with his dusty ragged robe.

"And it chose yes . . . if only because its choosing to do so might serve as an example to us when our time comes. The saying goes that 'it's a big galaxy'—but it's one of an uncountable number, and one lifetime is a minuscule fraction of the span of the universe. Nonetheless, there's room in one lifetime to do amazing things!

"It could have chosen not to be remembered, you know. It wanted not to be remembered, not even to have been heard of. It was itself no more than was Gregory Chart, who on scores of planets has cobbled together the foundations for true culture out of snippets and scraps, jokes and nursery rhymes and folklore! And to have found that one man among millions had already undertaken what it had needed millennia to accomplish . . .

"But that was its one lifetime, and it could not bear

to have nothing to mark its passing. Even a failure, so it reasoned, on the scale of the universe, might be better than oblivion.

"So, for the first time, we have seen a species pass away. It grew old. It had done its best. It wanted to be remembered for its best. And even if in the end it leaves no trace but a few poems, those will carry on, in their fashion."

He sat down.

There was silence for a while. Eventually the delegates, without a signal, began to rise from their desks and disperse; so too did the witnesses on the platform. Marc remained in his chair, feeling curiously weary, as though he had stood for a long time under a vast burden without realising how big it was until he had relinquished it.

He found, eventually, that Dr Lem was looking at him, and started up, apologising for his rudeness. But the old man brushed the words aside.

"What I want to know is this," he said. "How can a person as young as you understand so clearly what it is to be old?"

"Because Yan was old."

"Yes, it was . . . Once you understand what it is to be old, you can never recapture what it was like to be young. You realise that?"

"I think so."

"Do you resent it?"

"No. I feel there's a purpose to it. I feel there's a reason."

"Oh, come now! We at least aren't being whipped by some collective overlord towards a goal we can't imagine, as the Yanfolk were . . ."

Dr Lem's voice trailed away under Marc's steady gaze. He said at last, "*Are* we?"

"If we are," Marc said, "I hope neither you nor I will ever have to know. Because the purpose might turn out to be futile, mightn't it?"

"Yes," Dr Lem said, his eyes focused on a fearful future. "Yes, of course it might."

"Time will tell," Marc said. "And when it does, I shall refuse to listen."

He took Dr Lem's arm and began to lead him out of the hall.

About the Author

John Brunner was born in England in 1934 and educated at Cheltenham College. He sold his first novel in 1951 and has been publishing sf steadily since then. His books have won him international acclaim from both mainstream and genre audiences. His most famous novel, the classic *Stand On Zanzibar*, won the Hugo Award for Best Novel in 1969, the British Science Fiction Award, and the Prix Apollo in France. Mr. Brunner lives in Somerset, England.